*J*ERRY RAN HER FINGERTIPS lightly over the top of the trunk. A shiver ran through her. Her fingers seemed electrified. She swept them across again. Did she feel a design in the top? She bent her face closer and noticed that there was a pattern of little pinpricks. It was as if her fingertips had been dusted with iron filings and the pinpricks were the magnets drawing the ... ink. These were letters she was touching. She could deduce their shape. The initials must be SdL.

She lifted the latch. This time it was not silent, and the creak startled her. But the latch simply fell off into her hand. How long had it been since anyone had opened this trunk? Had Constanza lived ninety-four years and never opened it? Did this constitute some sort of trespassing? Jerry wondered. As she lifted its lid, she realized that this was beyond right or wrong.

Blood Secret

By Kathryn Lasky

HarperTrophy®
An Imprint of HarperCollinsPublishers

Blood Secret
Copyright © 2004 by Kathryn Lasky
All rights reserved. Printed in the United States of America.
No part of this book may be used or reproduced in any manner
whatsoever without written permission except in the case of
brief quotations embodied in critical articles and reviews. For
information address HarperCollins Children's Books, a division
of HarperCollins Publishers, 1350 Avenue of the Americas,
New York, NY 10019.
www.harperchildrens.com

Library of Congress Cataloging-in-Publication Data
Lasky, Kathryn.
Blood secret / by Kathryn Lasky.—1st ed.
p. cm.
Summary: Fourteen-year-old Jerry Luna, mute since her
mother's disappearance, is sent to her great-great-aunt
Constanza's house, where she discovers a trunk that draws her
into the world of her ancestors during the Spanish Inquisition.
ISBN-10: 0-06-000063-5 — ISBN-13: 978-0-06-000063-9
[1. Time travel—Fiction. 2. Aunts—Fiction. 3. Mute
persons—Fiction. 4. People with disabilities—Fiction.
5. Inquisition—Spain—Fiction. 6. Spain—History—Ferdinand
and Isabella, 1479–1516—Fiction. 7. New Mexico—Fiction.]
I. Title.
PZ7.L3274Bl 2004   2003022299
[Fic]—dc22

Typography by Henrietta Stern
❖
First Harper Trophy Edition, 2006

In memory of
Meredith Charpentier,
my friend,
my editor,
my navigator

—K.L.

Rim Rock, Colorado

IT WAS THE NOTHINGNESS that woke her up. It was like a hole beside her, as if she were on the edge of it and might fall in. Her mother had been there and then she wasn't. When they had gone to sleep that night in the tent, they were side by side in the big puffy double sleeping bag, all cozy and curled up together. They fit like spoons against each other. Now the space beside her was blank. She opened her eyes and looked into the darkness. Outside she could hear a few voices. They were camped near the place where the concert would be. A rock concert in a rock stadium. That was funny. She and her mom made jokes about it. They always got to concerts plenty early, days early, so her mom could set up her jewelry stuff and sell it.

Her mom must have had to go pee. She would be back soon. So Jerry waited and waited. Then she heard her mom's voice. At last, she thought, and the knots in her stomach dissolved. She got up on her knees and peeked out the little nylon screen square that served as the window. She saw her mom in the big shirt she wore to sleep in and barefoot. Then she saw her crouch down and crawl into the man's tent, the man named Jim who had sold her the stuff for the pipe she smoked. She watched transfixed. Her mom was naked under that shirt, and as she crawled in Jerry could see her mom's butt. She put her hand over her mouth. She thought she might cry. She thought she might shout, "Mom—your butt!" She didn't know what she might say. So she clamped her mouth shut and slammed her hand against it. She crumpled up into the sleeping bag. She wanted to dive right down to the foot of the bag, but then she wouldn't be able to breathe. Still she felt these sobs swelling up in her throat, so she bit into the puffy quilted squares to stifle the awful wet sounds.

"Jerry, what the hell? You've bitten right through this down sleeping bag. Lucky you didn't gag on the feathers, crazy little girl!" Sure enough, a little thread of down drifted lazily through the air close to the tent floor.

Her mother was back. It was dawn.

"Where've you been, Mom?"

"Just out visiting."

"Jim?"

"Now how'd you guess—you a little peeping tom? Peeping Jerry?"

Jerry didn't exactly get the joke. She *had* been peeping. "Huh?" Her mother nudged her. She didn't answer. She didn't want to say what she had seen— her mom's naked butt going into that tent. If she'd at least been wearing underpants! "Huh?" Her mom giggled and nudged her again. But Jerry didn't say anything.

This was the first time Jerry had swallowed words. But the silence was okay. Jerry was five. Over the next few years, it would become easier and easier to swallow the words.

Chapter 1

❖❖❖

THE SECOND TIME she had gone to the Catholic Charities home, when she was eight, it had been in Colorado, where her mother had disappeared. She was there almost a year. During that time she had thought of her mother every day. She had lit candles. The sisters had always told them at the home that the burning candle was a symbol of heart-felt prayer. Sister Norma had called it a vigil light and a sign of watchful waiting, a true act of devotion, and she had said it was appropriate for Jerry to light such a candle; it was like a light in the window for her mother, for a loved one's return, for her spiritual return. Jerry's mother, the nuns told her, could see the flame of the candle she had lit from heaven. You cannot call out to heaven, but the candle silent yet shining shows our love. It was like opening a window through which a soul could come. It seemed like magic. Jerry imagined a window with the shimmer of a candle reflected and herself holding that candle, waiting in front of the window, waiting for her mother's soul to hoist itself over the sill and through the window just where the flame shimmered. But the thing was that as soon as her mother stepped out of that window, she would no longer be just a soul. She would be real and she would be safe.

Jerry was patient. She could wait. She could wait a long time if she had to. So she had prayed and lit lots and lots of candles. She had tried to picture her mother dead in a coffin with lilies lying on top of it. She pictured herself kneeling by the coffin. But the problem was, of course, her mother was not for sure dead; she was missing and presumed dead. They had been hunting for her forever in the red rock country. And what help had Jerry been? None whatsoever because, when her mother disappeared, that was when Jerry had stopped speaking completely.

The state troopers had come, search teams, national guards, all to look for the mother of the little girl who was found wandering on the edge of a campground. But she couldn't speak. Someone at the campsite remembered her mother had said

5

something about going hiking. The mother had hung out with a lot of potheads and druggies and she didn't look well. No, not at all. So a search was started. But Jerry couldn't help them. She knew what her mother had been wearing that day. Her long skirt covered in violets. The ruffled pink blouse, a leather vest, and a big cowboy hat. But she couldn't tell them. She couldn't tell them about her mother's crinkly black hair with the seashells woven in, or the tattoos. She had one on her thigh and one on her belly that said "Hammerhead." She was going to get one that said "Jerry" and Jerry was going to get one that said "Millie" when they got to the good tattoo place in Arizona. But then her mother had just disappeared.

One day at the Catholic Charities home, Sister Norma had come in and said, "We must think, Jerry, that now for sure your mother is dead. It has been more than a year. I am going to have Monsignor Rafael say a mass for her. We shall buy you a new dress and I think, dear, this will help. And look, the Friends of Catholic Charities have all chipped in and we have made a donation to the Franciscan Mission Association here in Colorado." She handed Jerry a card. The outside of the card was linen, and on it inscribed in gold was a drawing of the Virgin sweeping open her cloak as if to enfold a Franciscan brother who held a cross. Inside it said, "To honor God and help spread his kingdom on Earth, a donation has been made to the Franciscan Mission Association on behalf of Mildred Moon, who will share for five years in the prayers and sacrifices of the conventual Franciscan Friars and will be remembered in their masses, including masses said over the tombs of St. Francis in Assisi and of St. Anthony in Padua."

"Isn't that lovely, dear? Don't you want to thank the sisters? Don't you want to say thank you?" She paused and fixed Jerry with a hard look. "Out loud?"

But Jerry had remained absolutely silent. Sister Norma made it sound very easy. You either were or you weren't dead. Nothing in between. This card made her mother for sure dead. The Franciscan brothers didn't pray for the "in betweens," only for the "for sures." What if it wasn't quite for sure? What if her mother wasn't really dead? What if Millie Moon came walking in and they had already bought the card? Would she have to give the card back? But Jerry liked the idea of praying to her mother in heaven. Her mother would be safe in heaven. And she, Jerry, got to carry a candle and hold a white lily.

She wasn't sure when it was that she realized the entire idea of cooking up a dead mother for her was part of Dr. Wright's notion of therapy. Dr. Wright visited the home once a week. He was sure that once Jerry had "closure," this would in some mysterious way help her to speak. Stupid! She would have no part of it. In fact, Jerry called Dr. Wright Dr. Wrong. In her mind, of course. She never spoke to Dr. Wrong. Not a word. It was very satisfying watching him trying to draw her out. He tried; they all tried. When the silence first came to her, she didn't realize she could do this with it, that she could make people almost hungry for her words. The silence was just nice, comforting. There was a coolness that would steal over her, a gray coolness that protected her from the glare out there. Even when they kept badgering her to speak, she could withdraw to that cool place. Silence was like dirt, good dirt. You could dig into it. You could bury stuff in it. She could bury the longing for her mother in this silence. Then one day she discovered that she had actually forgotten the sound of her own voice. She wasn't even sure if she missed the memory of her voice. So many years had passed now and with every year she buried the longing deeper, the memory of her voice deeper into the good dirt of the silence.

Jerry felt the nervousness of the woman behind the wheel as they drove down New Mexico Route 25. People were not good at being near stillness and silence. The nuns of course were the worst of all. Nuns were teachers and nurses. Their whole point in life was to teach and heal. They had tried their best with Jerry. She had failed them. She knew what she looked like to them. She looked cut. She looked as if she had a wound that sucked up words and bled silence. But psychologists and social workers weren't much better. And it was Jerry's stillness that unnerved Phyllis Wingfield. It was as if Jerry had become part of the car's upholstery, and she had never seen anything as inanimate as Jerry. So absolutely still. Jerry felt her stealing glances at her from behind those mirror-lens sunglasses she wore. She's probably wondering if I am real, real for sure alive, like Millie being real for sure dead. Or maybe she thinks I'm just a shadow on the seat.

The San Mateo exit came up. "Restrooms!"

Phyllis Wingfield exclaimed. "I think I'll stop. Jerry, do you need to stop?" Silence.

They pulled into the rest area's parking lot. Switching off the ignition, she asked again. "You sure you don't want to go? This is a pretty clean one, as I remember." Jerry stared straight ahead. "Well, I'll be back in a few minutes. I think they have snack machines. I'm having a cookie craving. I'll pick us up something." She reached for her wallet and left the briefcase open with Jerry's file peeking out the top.

Compliant . . . No organic involvement . . . Jerry always read her in-take forms. She had become so adept at it that she could read them upside down if she had to. Under "Antecedent Behavior" there was a short dash. She licked her finger and picked at the next page. Ah, the good old Functional Behavioral Assessment Matrix—comfortably blank except, of course, for the little boxes where they could check the rates of social engagement. The "Not Socially Engaged" box was filled in. There was a recommendation for a neuropsychological evaluation based on a previous clinical report, which was included. There wasn't time to read the report. The woman would be coming back any minute. Besides, Jerry knew what it would say. *Selective mutism, complete refusal to speak in social situations, high ability to understand spoken language, to read and to write,* or it might opt to call her silence *"elective mutism"*—that was the clinical term. It made it seem as if being mute was part of an exclusive club.

Jerry continued reading. *Exhibits extreme levels of anxiety when pressed to respond verbally or interact verbally. Otherwise compliant.* That was the single most-used word in any description of Jerry Moon.

Or was it Jeraldine de Luna or was it Jerafina Hammerhead or was it Jerrene Milagros? Her mother, Mildred, had a thing about names—and men, for that matter. She touched the crown of her head and then began picking and rubbing her hair as if she had an itch. But there was no itch. It was just a soothing gesture. She looked up. The woman was heading back. So she flipped to the cover page. There it was. She was Jeraldine de Luna, age fourteen, mother Mildred Milagros de Luna, father Hammerhead. Father deceased. Mother presumed dead. "Whatever!" The word hung as a silent mutter in her head. She stared forward through the car's windowpane.

Mirror Eyes was smiling broadly. How many times before had Jerry sat in a car and watched a state worker come toward her smiling, someone from some Department of Child Services with mirrored sunglasses? They all seemed to wear them.

"Have a cookie, Jerry?" Phyllis Wingfield peeled back the plastic on the packet and offered her one. Jerry gave a barely perceptible shake of her head.

She looked out the window as the landscape slid by in a blur of muted reds and dusky tans. No trees, just scrub stuff—clumps of snakeweed, needle grass, sagebrush. What grew out here in New Mexico was maybe the least interesting part of the scenery, Jerry thought. It was what had been that was fascinating. There was this strange geometry to the land. The mesas that rose like stacked pancakes must have been carved away by ten thousand winters of scouring blizzards, ten thousand springs of torrential rains. Even from the car Jerry could see a dust storm raging miles away, with whirlwinds scraping across shallow basins and sucking up red dust from one place to drop it in another. As they approached a deep bend in the road, a sign warned of falling rock from the cliffs.

She might see some of the ancient rock carvings.

There were Kokopelli figures all over the place out here. When she had been at the second Catholic Charities home here in New Mexico, there was a rock cliff on the grounds that showed the old flute player that the cave-dweller Indians from seven hundred years ago must have loved for his rowdiness. Kokopelli, with his hunched back and his spindly legs dancing to his own tune as he played his flute in the deep silence of the stone. The nuns took them up there for picnics sometimes. Up close, the red sandstone cliffs were not just red. There were stripes of color—pink, reddish purple. Purplish red, a cool gray. They were really layers of time. In the clear dry air they stood out perfectly— time translated into stone. Neat and organized and yet, as the sign warned, it could crush you. Jerry imagined a boulder breaking off from the cliff and crashing through the roof of the car. She and Mirror Eyes squashed flat under a million years of time— surely, surely dead.

"Jerry, this aunt—she is actually, according to our records, your great-great-aunt, Constanza de Luna—sounds like a lovely woman. She's a baker. A very good one. Apparently supplies lots of restaurants in the Albuquerque area, as well as some country clubs. You will have your own room and bathroom, and the high school is walking distance. Now, you're a freshman, aren't you?"

No nod this time. "And I understand that except for your reluctance to talk, you are a good student. Indeed, your last school report spoke of your being fluent in reading and writing Spanish as well as English." She waited; still no response. "That's wonderful!" Jerry began having the funny feeling in her throat. It happened whenever anyone got hot and bothered about the talking thing. Thank God they were pulling into the drive now.

Chapter 2

✦✦✦

A TRUCK HAD JUST driven in ahead of them. It was white, and in bright yellow swoopy letters were the words "Constanza Delivers." In smaller print it said, "Finest in Southwestern Breads and Pastries." There was a toll-free number.

The door opened, and from the shadows of the truck's cab one very long leg unfolded. A thin cotton dress hiked up at the knee revealed that the leg was not only long but also scaled and blistered. The other leg followed. The woman stepped to the ground and straightened up. She was more than six feet tall, thin as a twig and straight as a cactus needle. Her dress swirled about her in little gusts, sometimes clinging to her thighs hardly thicker than arms. She was old, that was for sure. Her hair, white as bleached bones, was pulled straight back in a knot. She reached in the truck and slapped on a raggedy hat, the kind the old Navajo men sometimes wore. Tall crown, flat brim, no curl to it like a Stetson or cowboy hat.

Mirror Eyes was stepping out of the car. She shook hands with the lady, whose face was now cast in the shadow of her hat's brim. Jerry's eyes traveled beyond them to the yard. Hard dirt packed with horno bread ovens popping out of the ground like a ghetto of giant beehives. Beyond the hornos was the low adobe house, a rough wood door painted pale blue, odd-shaped windows punching the walls that watched like blank eyes in the hot noonday sun.

A sudden shadow slid across the car window and into her lap. The old lady had come right up to her side and leaned in. Jerry gasped. It was not only that she hadn't been expecting her to do this, but also her face was so close, and it loomed dark and somehow fantastic in the window frame.

"You want to get out, child?" the woman asked.

Jerry moved her hand to the door handle. She paused, opening her eyes wide, and peered directly into the woman's face. Above her upper lip was a hedge of thin, crimped, vertical lines. A radiation of similar lines as fine as cobwebs spread from the far corners of her eyes to her temples. Jerry had seen old people before, their faces creased and gouged into deep crevices or crumpled into fleshy pouches, but she had never seen a face like this. Dark and tawny as leather, the tissue paper–thin skin had crinkled into a fine tracery. The eyes were so heavily hooded that it was impossible to see much of the white. And was the iris black or was it a deep amber?

"Come along, child. Might be March, but it's hot enough in this car to bake bread, and I don't need another oven in my yard." A ragged snort tore from her throat as she looked up and gestured.

Mirror Eyes had already gotten her suitcase out of the trunk and was handing Jerry's aunt a folder of papers. She got back into the car and leaned out the window cheerfully. "Good-bye, Jerry. It's been nice . . . ," but her voice dwindled off as she started the engine.

Her aunt's shadow grew longer as Jerry followed her along a stone-edged path to the house. She was careful not to step out of that silhouette.into the white light. The shadow stretched and grew narrow, and Jerry pressed her arms to her sides. Then the shadows of the roofline of the house began to reach out for them. Constanza stopped for a moment and looked toward the ovens. Heat rippled off them in waves, distorting the air.

For some odd reason, perhaps not so odd, Jerry thought of Hansel and Gretel, but she made her feet go forward in the shadow of this aunt. At least they told her this old lady *was* her aunt. But you never really knew anything for sure. Dead for sure, alive for sure, an aunt for sure.

The next morning when Jerry woke, she watched the light slide through the deep-cut window like a thief stealing the shadows one by one from Jerry's bedroom. She could smell the bread baking, and if she looked out she could see the humped profiles of the hornos' shadows stretching across the cook yard. When the shadows started to shrink, that was when the first batch of bread was ready to come out and that was when everything smelled the best. The smell swirled through the yard, and even the tumbleweed that reeled by seemed to pause for a second or two as if not wanting to leave. Then in the afternoon the shadows would begin to stretch long again.

This was what Jerry did for her first few days at her Aunt Constanza's. She sought shadows through following light. She had her favorite places both indoors and out. It was an old-style adobe. Scattered at odd angles across the earthen floors in the living room were colorful woven rugs. There wasn't very much furniture at all. No sofa, just a banco, a kind of bench, where the thick adobe had been cut away from the wall to offer a deep niche for sitting. Because the house was so empty—no knickknacks, just a kitchen table, a low coffee table, a few chairs—it was as if the light and the shadow were the real furniture.

Jerry fit in a strange way. Her silence matched the shadows. She could slip between the dark and the light, slide between the swirling motes of dust busy in the shafts of sun, and disturb nothing.

The light entered the house in many different ways because of the windows' odd shapes. Some were shuttered and some not. She walked outside, where the shadows of clouds cast pictures on the flat, scrubby land—a buffalo charging, a rabbit with wings, an angel with a rabbit's head, a hunchback caped and hooded creeping across the landscape. Shadow characters in shadow stories. She could feel the shadows and not simply their coolness. They had a weight. Maybe in the same way that time was fixed in the layers of stone, shadows out here carried their own histories.

Indoors by late afternoon the last of the sunlight slipped from the banco, and the violet grayness of the early evening began to gather in the rooms.

Constanza did not seem bothered in the least by the fact that Jerry didn't talk. Constanza didn't talk much herself. She might have said three or four dozen sentences to her in the first two days Jerry had been there. Tonight Jerry had set the table for dinner after Constanza returned from her late deliveries. Constanza had told her to turn on the "range," as she called the inside oven, for the roast. Jerry had just about begun to think that Constanza was a vegetarian. There had been no meat at any meal so far. The first night a vegetable stew with the delicious flatbread—the morning's last batch—and salad. Last night a fritatta. But now a roast and it smelled good. She hoped that Constanza would serve one of the fancy little pastries she had made as a special order for the country club. They were puffy little golden shells filled with cream and preserved apricots from Constanza's own tree. In the center of each one she had set a sparkling raspberry. When Jerry saw the pastries sitting out on the counter, she almost gasped. They looked like jewels. . . . Almost gasped. It was as if that sound somehow died in her throat. She had been sitting on the stool and watching as Constanza packed them. She had made nests of tissue paper in neat little white boxes and then set them in, six to a box. Jerry had watched Constanza's long, bony fingers. The knuckles knobbed with arthritis, her hands placed the shells so carefully. Her fingers and hands were whiter than the rest of her. It was as if she could never get rid of the flour. It had in some way been absorbed into her skin. After the pastries were boxed and tied with string, she took a label from a spool fastened to the counter. The labels were oval and printed in the same swoopy writing: "Constanza Delivers."

The little tartlets were so different from the sheet cakes that they always served at the Catholic Charities homes or the state-run homes for kids like Jerry. Everything here was different. Not just the food. The floors were different. No linoleum. Linoleum smelled funny, she suddenly realized, and that smell was not here. The living room floor at Constanza's was earth, dirt, and it felt cool coming up through your feet. The kitchen floor was wood. There were no steam tables in Constanza's kitchen with metal pans set in them and giant spoons to shovel out the food for lines of kids. Constanza served food in ceramic casseroles and dishes.

Jerry had wanted to help Constanza with the tartlets. She liked the process of packing the sweet little gemstones. She found the rhythm of the small tasks strangely comforting, but of course she could not ask and she was afraid to simply start helping. So she sat silently and looked.

"Ah, the table's set," Constanza said as she came into the kitchen from her deliveries. "Thank you, child." She stopped abruptly as she untied her hat. "I shouldn't call you child. I must stop that. You are fourteen. I'll try and remember to call you Jerry."

At least Constanza did not say, as teachers so often did, "Now do you prefer Jerry or Jeraldine?" She never could answer that one. She always just shrugged a bit. "And you, when you like, may call me Aunt Constanza or just Constanza or Connie if you must. I come when called." And that was the first time Jerry saw Constanza smile. She also noticed that her aunt was missing one tooth, the third from the left of her front teeth. It was a dark little gap that only the smile could reveal.

Constanza had just finished slicing the roast

when Jerry got up to get herself a glass of milk. "Oh no, Jerry!" Constanza said as she sat down with the milk. "No, you can't have that!" What had she done? Jerry looked quite confused. Every other night she'd been allowed to pour herself a glass of milk. "Don't you know it's terrible for your digestion?" Constanza continued. "To drink milk with meat, especially red meat. Oh, you'll be sick as a dog. And tomorrow's your first day of school."

Jerry had never heard of such a thing in her life. She knew darn well that it wouldn't hurt her. She went and put the milk back and got herself some water. Now as they sat over their roast, Constanza looked up. "I'm going to the seven o'clock mass this evening. I was too busy with those tarts this morning to make it. You're welcome to come. But I want to get there early."

Jerry felt her head nod slightly, almost mechanically.

Jerry watched Constanza disappear into the confession booth. She wondered what possible sins this old lady could confess. It seemed like a lifetime ago to Jerry since she had last seen people go to confession. It was probably the first time she had been at the Catholic Charities home in Santa Rosa. That was before her mother had disappeared but after she became too sick to take care of Jerry. She wondered what she would have confessed back then when she could still talk, if indeed she had been old enough to go to confession. Probably something to do with envy. Envy of other girls. She had arrived at the home with her peculiar clothes. The long flowered skirts that her mother liked to dress her in and the lace-up hiking boots and the frilly blouses. Everyone else had been wearing normal clothes: jeans, cutoffs, T-shirts. Well, yes, she did have her own Harley Davidson T-shirt. But that probably had more to do with her mother's yearning for Hammerhead than anything to do with her.

There were only four other people in the church for the evening mass and only one other aside from Constanza took confession. It was a nice church— very small. Jerry doubted if there was room for more than fifty worshippers. It was adobe, and there was only one stained-glass window. But darkness had already fallen and there was not enough moonlight, so the colors seemed drained from the glass and the Virgin looked almost sickly, as a woman might look if she had suddenly turned pale under her makeup. The painted surface was still there, but the blood beneath the skin gone. There was an arrangement of dried grasses and a few branches from some flowering tree. The tall, thick tapers in the candlesticks were guttering down, and their last flickerings cast antic shadows on the adobe walls.

Constanza came out of the confessional and knelt in prayer. When Jerry saw Constanza rise, she put her rosary beads in her pocket and followed her aunt. At the door of the church, the priest stood waiting for them.

"Jerry, this is Padre Hernandez." Jerry stood there saying nothing. She might have nodded slightly. Padre Hernandez took her hand. "Your aunt tells me that you're quiet." Jerry pressed her lips together into a line that could have meant agreement or "so it goes." He continued holding her hand in his. His hand was large and warm. The skin rough. She felt a callus at the edge of his palm. "You know, Jerry, silence is not merely the absence of words. It can indicate the presence of something as well. You are welcome to confess even without words. God does not need to hear words to listen to a heart speaking." This time Jerry nodded again, twice. He squeezed her hand and then released it.

They walked out of the church to where the

truck was parked. Constanza gave a big sigh as she got her keys out. "Tired. So tired." Then she turned to Jerry. "You drive?" She held out the keys. Jerry stopped and looked at her aunt. Her mouth opened to say "What?" But the word remained within. Constanza looked at her. "I know. I know. You don't have a license. That doesn't matter. When I was a girl, they didn't even have driver's licenses. I was younger than you when I started. Get in now." She thrust the keys into Jerry's hands. Aunt Constanza's instructions were brief and to the point. She showed Jerry the gears. Let her try them to find the positions. She explained about the clutch, and then they were off.

"Press in the clutch. Let up easy. Don't ride that damn thing like a nun. You've never seen a bad driver until you've seen Sister Evangelina. Not much traffic tonight. I'll take you out when there's more so you can learn how to switch lanes. Nothing worse than getting stuck behind some pokey old lady driver."

Jesus! Jerry thought. So she was probably with the only old lady speed demon in America. Jerry actually felt her heart race as she imagined trying to pass one of those immense semis, a sixteen wheeler!

They rode on in silence for a few more minutes. Then Constanza seemed to peer forward. "Now I don't mean to get you nervous." Jerry clenched the wheel and felt her hands begin to perspire. "But we're coming up on a stretch where a deer can bounce out of the brush." Jerry swallowed. What was she supposed to do? "Now, you'll see their eyes first. They just kind of *boing* out at you all red and fiery. And they don't move. See, that's the problem. They get kind of hypnotized by your car lights. So you have to be prepared to swerve." What? Jerry thought. This was horrifying. "You slam into a deer. Well, you can total the truck. Deer won't be much good either." Constanza snorted.

Five minutes later they pulled into the drive and Jerry turned off the ignition.

"So there." Aunt Constanza smacked her lips together. Jerry could not tell if this was an expression of approval or a statement of fact, the fact that they had arrived. Aunt Constanza climbed down from the truck and slammed the door.

When they were in the kitchen, Constanza sat down with a thump on a kitchen chair. "Nothing's as hard as it seems." Jerry assumed she was referring to the driving. "Day after tomorrow I have a big delivery to the country club, the snooty one on the northeast side of the city. We have to take the highway. Good practice. Lots of traffic. Passing!" Constanza said almost gleefully.

Constanza got up and listened to her answering machine and wrote down the new orders that had come in. She fixed Jerry and herself cups of hot chocolate. They had just sat down, each lost in her own thoughts, when they happened to look up from their hot chocolate. Each had just raised her hand to the top of her head and begun to rub the hair. It was the precisely identical nature of the gesture that stunned each of them. It was as if Jerry and Constanza were, despite the years, for one brief moment mirror images of each other. "Oh, dear child, don't do that. You have the same bad habit as me. Look, you want the top of your head to look like mine?" Costanza tipped her head forward. Jerry saw that right at the crown the center part widened and seemed in fact to dissolve into a patch of pink covered by a few white strands. "You twist your hair, don't you? Yes, I did too as a child and that is why my mother parted it in the middle and made me wear braids. But if I couldn't twist it, I would rub it. My abuela had a bald patch on top that was big as a saucer." Jerry suddenly wondered how old Constanza was. How long had it taken her to get this bald patch that was, if not as big as a saucer, at least as big as the well in the saucer in which a cup set? How many years of twisting and rubbing had it taken? She didn't want to go bald. She curled her hand into a fist and fought the urge to raise it again.

Jerry rested her chin on her fist and looked at Constanza, who was studying her sheet of orders. Was there more than just this silly old habit that connected them? Did they look alike in any way? Constanza was so tall and skinny. Jerry was short and—she hated the word—*stocky*, but she was. Constanza had Indian blood. You could tell it immediately. And although Jerry had a dark olive complexion, there was absolutely nothing olive in the darkness of Constanza's face. There was a deep, deep reddish brown to the darkness. Were they of the same blood? Carve away the pudginess of her own face, were the bones underneath it at all the same? It wasn't just Constanza's high cheekbones, however, that indicated Indian blood. There was something else. Maybe it was the slope of her forehead, the sharpness of her nose. Constanza's nose sat as bold as a knife-back ridge on her face. When

Jerry thought of her own face, it seemed kind of squashy and soft in comparison. Her mother had had sort of a sharp nose, but it was short and fragile, perched on her face like one of those teeny tiny handles from one of those teeny tiny teacups, and her mother was about as fragile as a teacup too. She was always breaking her bones, breaking her bones and breaking her nerves. She talked a lot about her nerves, and her feelings and her emotions. Jerry listened.

"I suppose," Constanza said, "you're a bit nervous about starting school tomorrow. I always rub my head when I get nervous. I'll walk with you tomorrow and show you the way. It's an easy walk. I have to go anyway to sign some health forms or something."

Without thinking, Jerry raised her hand again to her head. She wasn't used to this. It made her uneasy to have someone fussing about her in this way. It wasn't like the nuns. And it wasn't like the social workers. And it sure wasn't like her mother. If anything, she would have been the one walking her mother to school.

Jerry got up to get the broom and began to sweep the kitchen floor. The door to the yard was open and she had just started to sweep the dirt over its threshold when Constanza's hand, like a claw, suddenly grabbed the broom from her. Jerry gasped. The suddenness of Constanza's gesture had frightened her. She could not imagine what she had done. Then, gently, Constanza spoke.

"No, child, never out the door. Always sweep the dirt to the center of the room and then pick it up with a dustpan and put it in the trash." Then, as if to apologize or perhaps explain, she added, "Just a silly old superstition, I guess."

Jerry bit her bottom lip and watched as Constanza bent down with a dustpan and collected the crumbs. A breeze came in through the open door and picked up a remaining few in a small gust and sucked them over the threshold into the night. What happens now? Jerry wondered.

Chapter 3

❖❖❖

JERRY THOUGHT that she and Constanza must have been quite a sight. The mute girl in her unfashionably long skirt that had once been one half of some mother-daughter matching ensemble that her own mother had gotten up for them, and the old lady in her Navajo hat and tall walking stick. Of course Jerry's skirt was not nearly as long as it had once been. She had grown a lot since then, but it still looked dumb. Unfortunately the waist had an elastic waistband and the nuns kept letting the seams out and the hem down. It was as if Jerry could never outgrow or get away from this skirt, or for that matter any of the ugly clothes that came out of the homes' charity bins. She had actually borrowed a work shirt of Constanza's to wear over the skirt, which diminished to some degree the stupid *Little House on the Prairie* look that her mother had loved.

Jerry did not like to think much about her mother. She had managed not to for a while, but wearing these clothes brought unpleasant thoughts. Her mother—Moon Lady, as she sometimes called herself—was a fashion schizophrenic. She either dressed like a Plains Indian in buckskin, beads, and feathers or in her *Little House on the Prairie* clothes. Jerry's mother had been nuts for Laura Ingalls Wilder. She had been nuts for a lot of things— Harleys, guys who rode Harleys, white zinfandel, grass, and of course her dolls. How could Jerry forget those damn dolls that her mother dragged with her everywhere. She didn't like to think about the dolls.

She distracted herself now by trying to keep within Constanza's shadow. She was tipping out of it, though. She watched the shadow of her aunt's hat slide across the shadow of a cactus. There was a split second when her aunt's shadow and the cactus's and her own dissolved into one black pool in the morning sun.

As they walked into the school, Jerry kept her eyes down because she was simply too embarrassed to look up and see the other kids staring at them.

Constanza asked where the office was.

The principal came out as soon as they were announced. "Oh yes, Ms. de Luna, we were expecting you and your niece. Actually the guidance counselor is waiting in his office for you now. And I believe you have all the paperwork?"

"Paperwork?" Constanza said. "Oh, you mean Jerry's records."

"Yes, yes, the Department of Child Services is supposed to send it, but you know bureaucracies." Constanza nodded. Jerry could not imagine that her aunt knew bureaucracies at all. Jerry knew bureaucracies! She'd been through them all: Department of Child Services, Catholic Charities, something called Helping Hand, a state and federally funded program. They were led into the counselor's office. On the glass was the name Henry Gilroy. A thin little man came out from behind his desk. "Welcome, Jerry. Welcome to Juan Lopez High School. Good morning, Ms. de Luna, a great fan of your bread, great fan." Mr. Gilroy offered them a seat and Constanza handed him the papers. He put on some black-framed glasses that looked much too heavy for his face. In fact, with his thin, pale yellow hair and small oval face, Mr. Gilroy reminded Jerry of a melon seed.

"Well, well." Mr. Gilroy seemed to be talking to himself in a low voice as he glanced over the papers. He looked up brightly at Jerry and said welcome a few more times. Finally Constanza said, "She's quiet." Mr. Gilroy raised one nearly transparent eyebrow and looked down at the sheet in front of him. He must be looking now at the part about elective mutism, Jerry thought, and he must be thinking that her aunt's remark was the understatement of the century. "Yes, indeed, but it does not seem to have impaired your academic experience. You'll be taking geometry. Oh yes, of course. And then you will be taking your social studies unit. And then English literature and a life science requirement. Most freshman take the biology course and then the health and hygiene course." Constanza nodded as if she was as completely familiar with the freshman curriculum as any bread dough recipe.

"And that about does it except for an elective. There's art, ceramics, photography, sewing." Jerry raised her hand slightly. "Sewing, does that interest you, Jerry?" She nodded slightly.

"That's a good choice," Constanza interjected. "I'm going to take her to buy some new clothes. But it would be nice if she could make something that she would really like."

"Well, terrific. Now I'm going to call one of the freshman girls who has a similar schedule, and she'll be your guide. Show you about the place."

Why am I pressing my lips together? Jerry thought as the guidance counselor introduced her to Sinta Garcia. I want to talk. But the words won't come out. They are just sucked away. Sucked up like the dust in those whirlwinds. Please! Please let this girl understand. Maybe they had told her. Maybe Sinta came from a long line of mutes— selective mutes—and had been the first one to speak. Maybe this was in fact the exclusive club, and that was why Sinta had been selected as her guide in school.

She looked at her, trying not to stare. Sinta was very tiny and compact. Not stocky. She had a very stylish asymmetrical haircut with bangs that flopped over perfectly to one side. There was something slightly Asian about her eyes. Her skin was not perfect. She had one zit on her chin and another coming on her cheek. But she was pretty.

"Well, let's go!" Sinta said cheerfully. Too cheerful. She's faking it, Jerry thought, and followed Sinta.

Their first class was geometry. Luckily Mr. Kolberg, the geometry teacher, kept them late so they had to run to health and hygiene. There wasn't time really to talk to anyone. A few rushed introductions that Jerry could nod her way through. They slid into their seats with Sinta whispering about how this was the stupidest, most boring class in the world and that they only talked about washing your hands after going to the bathroom and before eating the seven basic foods and they couldn't talk about sex and condoms and AIDS because the school board said no.

Of course the class was not that boring to Jerry because she worried about lunch period, which would happen next. "Have you ever heard of anything so ridiculous. Lunch at ten forty-five. Like you're really hungry. No one eats. They just talk," Sinta said blithely as they made their way to the cafeteria. "Get something now that you can sneak a bite of later when you really do get hungry. Actually the grilled cheese sandwiches don't taste that bad cold. Grilled cheese and a Twinkie usually do me. Quiet food, if you know what I mean. Not crunchy or crackly like an apple or chips."

They sat at a table with mostly girls. Sinta

introduced her and once more she nodded and gave a small almost smile. "She's in sewing with us, Jessie," Sinta said to a girl across from her. Jessie seemed not to pay attention. Another girl asked her a question and Jerry just shook her head no. It was funny with kids. They always caught on right away that she just didn't talk. No explanation necessary and that was it. But it didn't make it more comfortable. She hated herself all the more. She hated that they got her so quickly. That she couldn't change it with them. She had sat at so many lunch tables so silent for so many years. The kids didn't taunt her. They just forgot she was there. She just became—what?—Quiet food—a cold grilled cheese, a Twinkie. On the outside she was very silent and would grow more and more still just like in the cars with all the mirror eyes, but inside everything raced. Words stormed; they beat themselves bloody in her head. Funny, it hadn't been this way in the beginning. It had been cool and safe. When had the silence turned?

Lunch lasted seventeen minutes. It felt like seventeen hours.

"Your aunt is Constanza Delivers? Wow!" Sinta exclaimed as the truck pulled up at the end of school. Jerry nodded and smiled. It wasn't a Harley, but she supposed it had its own kind of style. "We love her bread."

Jerry wanted to say, "You should taste her pastries," but as usual she just stood very still and said nothing. Sinta walked up to the truck with Jerry. "Hi, Miss de Luna. Jerry needs to buy about two-and-a-half yards of fabric for sewing class and some thread." Constanza nodded. There was an awkward pause. "Well, good-bye," Sinta said. She waved and walked off toward the school bus.

First they went and picked out the fabric. Then Constanza turned to Jerry and looked her up and down. "You need some new clothes. Let's go in here." She nodded toward a store with a sign that said Southwestern Fashions. Constanza walked up to a salesgirl. "This is my niece. I know nothing about what kids wear these days. Could you help her get some stuff for school?"

"Of course," the young woman said.

"Great. I'll go to the hardware store, Jerry, and meet you back here in half an hour at the cash register."

Jerry felt panic rise in her. The salesgirl was already battering her with questions. Did she want jeans? Skirts? T-shirts? Somehow Jerry spotted a skirt rack and walked to it. She started picking out several skirts. The salesgirl got her and stopped asking questions and instead started to give answers. "There are some cute shirts that go with that. And oh, these new pants and blazer are really cool."

It was when Jerry was trying on the jeans in the dressing room that she realized that never in her life had she tried on clothes in a dressing room alone without her mother. This was new. There was no one saying that this will look "adorable" on you and really meaning it looked exactly like something her mother wore. And of course usually her mother didn't buy stuff for Jerry in stores. Usually her mother took something of her own and cut it down to fit Jerry.

Jerry had taken in a pile of jeans, some nice corduroy trousers with a matching blazer, two cropped tops, a couple of shirts, a sweater, three skirts—short skirts that didn't drag in the dust! She tried on a short skirt first. This looks good, she thought, really good. She turned slowly and watched her reflection in the mirror. She blinked. It was only a split second, but she saw two reflections in the mirror—hers in the slim, short, denim skirt and her mother's in a long flower-print one smiling her sweet, spacey smile. Within the split of that second, it was as if Jerry had fallen into a deep crack in time. The voice came like a wind from a distant canyon.

"You made a picture of me in that long skirt, sweetie, on the Harley. Remember how careful you were to put on the helmet, and you even drew in my eyelashes? Remember you, me, and Dad on the motorcycle all the time?"

And then the words stormed silently inside Jerry's brain. *"No, Mom, you don't remember. It was not 'all the time.' Dad left when I was what? Three weeks old, but we always tried to say a month. Remember The Day Hammerhead Left. Now go away."* Jerry stared into the mirror and willed her mother's reflection away.

There was indeed a time when Jerry loved that story her mother had told her about riding on a Harley when she was two days old, leaving the hospital after she was born. All three of them rode off on the big shiny motorcycle. Therefore Jerry might be the youngest kid ever to have ridden on a Harley

Davidson. That counted for something! In the first grade, when they had to draw a picture and tell the teacher a story about it, Jerry had drawn a picture of a big old Harley—a hog, that's what the bikers called them—and she had a lady sitting on the back in a pretty dress and a helmet painted with flowers. Wrapped up in blankets was a little baby wearing a little baby helmet. And big eyelashes. Jerry had been one of those kids who never forgot to draw in the eyelashes. She did the whole bit, really. No little round o's for eyes. Her eyes had irises and pupils. Sometimes she made the lashes spiky and sometimes long and curly and sexy. "But you've forgotten the driver, Jerry?" the teacher had said. "Who's driving the motorcycle?" Silence. "Your dad?" "I guess." That was in the days when she still talked. She just preferred not to talk about her dad because then she would have to explain how he disappeared three weeks after she was born and how her mother never stopped talking about it. The Day Hammerhead Left—it sounded like a title for a bad movie trying to be an epic. "Why don't you put in the driver?" the teacher suggested. "Yes, ma'am." Jerry drew in a stick figure. But she was in a hurry and just put dots in for eyes, then at the last minute decided to add some lashes. Poor driver looked naked without them.

By the time she met her aunt at the cashier, she had two pairs of jeans, a skirt, several tops, and the pants with the matching corduroy blazer. She began to unfold them to show Constanza.

"Oh, child, don't ask me. What do I know about fashion? I'm over ninety."

Jerry heard herself gasp. She knew her aunt was old but not that old. How much over ninety? she wondered.

Then Constanza, as if reading her mind, said, "Ninety-four and a half."

Jerry opened her mouth. "A half?" but the words had been spoken by the sales clerk at the register.

"Oh, it's nothing so astonishing. Women in our family live well into their hundreds."

Chapter 4

JERRY HAD WORN the denim skirt to school the next day, but she had not tried on any of the clothes in front of the mirror. Now she put on the blazer with the faded jeans. It was silly, she knew, but she was almost scared to look in the mirror. She didn't want to see her mother's reflection. She knew it was stupid. It had only been a momentary thing. It wasn't even like a ghost thing. It was actually more her mother's voice in her head than a real image. She had read once that a person's memory for voice is a lot more vivid than their memory for face, and that when a loved one is lost it is easier to retrieve the sound of that person's voice than her face. But she had not retrieved the memory of her own voice.

Now she heard the rasping outside in the cook yard. Her aunt was raking out the ashes from the cold hornos in preparation for the next day's fire. It was a nice sound. One that she listened for at this time in the late afternoon. Cautiously she slid her eyes slowly up before she looked directly in the mirror.

This was the coolest blazer. Jerry turned and looked at herself from the back. It fit great. The corduroy was the color of tobacco. With the washed jeans it was perfect. And she loved her new running shoes. She had never owned a pair of running shoes, not even those little Keds sneakers that kids always wear. She looked at herself steadily in the mirror and lifted her heavy, dark hair. That was it! She had to wear her hair up. She looked so much better. Taller, less stocky. Now if only she could talk. It was Friday night and Sinta had invited her to go to a party. It was a party with older kids. There would probably be beer, Sinta said, but she didn't drink . . . well, sometimes . . . but it would be fun. She had gotten through the week all right, especially with Sinta at her side. Sinta had come over after school two days in a row and they had cut out their projects for sewing class together. Jerry felt comfortable with Sinta. But she didn't want to monopolize her. It was tough being monopolized by someone who couldn't speak. No, there was no way that she could go to that party. She didn't want Sinta to feel responsible for her. Jerry knew what it was like feeling responsible for someone. She had spent a lifetime feeling responsible for her mother. But it wasn't only that. Jerry didn't kid herself. No. She was a freak. And freaks didn't go to parties. She shook her head no.

Jerry suddenly tried to imagine the sound of her own voice. She tried to imagine herself speaking to Sinta. She closed her eyes as she stood in front of the mirror and attempted to visualize the words. But they didn't come out as words, not letters, not sounds, just some amorphous shapes, almost transparent like bubbles. They floated off noiselessly, leaving her throat dry. Did her voice really sound like what she thought it must have been? It had to have changed. It had been so long. She felt the funny feeling beginning in her throat. Why wasn't it comfortable anymore? Now it felt as if the words couldn't get past her throat. She wasn't really gagging. No, it was more as if there were a trap down there.

She cut off her thoughts and turned away from the mirror. It was almost dinnertime. Just before she walked out of her bedroom, she stole another glance at herself in the mirror. She must hunt around in Constanza's kitchen for a rubber band to put her hair up.

She stopped short as she came into the living room. What was that old lady doing now? Constanza's back was to her and she had changed her dress before dinner. Something she had never done. On her head was a shawl, perhaps silk. It looked old but expensive. Her aunt was standing in front of two candlesticks and she had obviously just lighted the candles.

Constanza turned around. She seemed surprised to see Jerry there. "Oh! I'm usually alone when I do this." The old lady's mouth settled into a grim line. Jerry felt as if she had indeed intruded on some private ceremony. Constanza seemed to read the question in Jerry's face. "It's to remember the death of Christ. Especially important to do it during Lent." Even if Jerry could speak, she felt it was maybe something she shouldn't ask about. Her aunt was strange. Leave it at that.

The candles stood on a table in front of a window. In the distance were the Sangre de Cristo Mountains. At this hour, however, they did not show the blood tinge of their name but were the color of old bruises against the sky. In the last flare of the setting sun, smoldering clouds streaked with lavender gathered above the mountains. What her aunt had just said made no sense to Jerry. She had heard of giving up things for Lent, and she knew that when she was at the Catholic Charities homes the sisters spoke to them about performing an act of penance during Lent, and that on Lenten Fridays no meat was served; but she had never heard of this candle routine. How did abstinence or penitence fit with lighting candles? There were good things cooking, that was for sure. She would have offered to set the table, but it was already set. A fresh cream-colored cloth had replaced the oilcloth. The good pottery that had been displayed on the shelves in the living room was now on the kitchen table, and there were flowers in a ceramic vase. Why all the fuss? she wondered.

Constanza came into the kitchen. From the oven she took out a pumpkin that had been baking. "Can you put together a salad, Jerry? The lettuce is washed."

Jerry moved off toward the refrigerator. The baked pumpkin smelled delicious. Just before they sat down, Constanza said, "If you want milk, you can get it. No meat in this pumpkin dish, you know, because of Lent. Just blue-cornmeal dumplings, peppers, and carrots. I think I'll have a bit of wine."

There was something special about this dinner. Jerry could tell just by the way Constanza ate, handled her fork, and shook out her napkin on her lap. Yes, a cloth napkin. At the other meals they had always had paper ones. But even if Jerry had had a voice, she would not have known the words to use to ask the questions. There seemed to be at the very heart of this dinner something so mysterious, so elusive as to defy words. It was more than a mystery, really. It seemed as if it might be a web of some sort that could ensnare them. There was something almost ritualistic in the way Constanza lifted the wineglass to her mouth. Ritualistic and at the same time mechanical.

They were wrapped in silence. The shadows began to gather in the corners of the room. There was tranquility, a peacefulness that was deep as the dirt, deep as silence. They watched the color drain from the sky outside. The sun had set perhaps twenty minutes before. The mountains had turned a cold purple, the clouds above a steely gray.

"The trapdoor spiders come out now," Constanza said suddenly. "If we go out we might see one. They hunt in the twilight." Constanza began to get up. Was she going out to see spiders or get dessert? Jerry got up and followed her aunt into the cook yard. As they passed by the hornos, she could still feel their heat, despite the chilliness of the evening.

"Ah, there's one now. See!" Constanza pointed down. Then, folding herself like one of those collapsible beach chairs, she crouched close to the ground. Her knees made sharp points under the fabric of her dress. "See what cunning little builders they are." She pointed at a piece of earth the size of a postage stamp that had begun to jiggle. "That's the trapdoor. It's made of silk and mud. Even the hinges are made of silk. And sometimes there is a second trapdoor farther down in the burrow. The burrows are lined with silk as well. Clever?" Constanza looked up, her eyes bright with this small marvel. "And you know, here in the cook yard they always seem to build their little traps within about two feet of a horno." The smell from the last batch of flatbread was still lingering in the yard. A little burrow lined with silk and filled with the scent of baking bread, very comfortable, Jerry thought.

Constanza looked directly into Jerry's eyes as the

two knelt watching the spider pry open the lid. "Yes, a nice situation for a spider."

"I hope they never get into your bread." Jerry spoke softly. The words simply slipped out. Constanza's hand began to tremble. They looked at each other.

"Oh, I never worry about that. I don't think they'd like the yeast, at least not the kind I use for the flatbread." Constanza turned her head away and looked at the ground as if searching for another spider or trapdoor.

I hope they never get into your bread. . . . I hope they never get into your bread. . . . The sound of her voice speaking continued to hum softly in Jerry's ears. As they sat down again at the table, the memory of her voice hovered in the room as well. She saw the words now hiding in dark corners, crawling into cracks.

"I was thinking about your sewing project for school," Constanza said. "I think in the root cellar there's an old sewing machine someplace. It's really old, not electric but with a treadle." Jerry looked up, her eyes questioning. "You know, the kind you have to work with your foot, pumping the foot piece back and forth."

Jerry nodded. It sounded good to her. The

machines in school went so fast. She always felt as if she were on a horse that might run away any minute.

"You can go down there. Take a flashlight, though, because there is only one lightbulb hanging from a cord. I don't think the machine is that heavy. With Sinta's help you could get it up here, or Father Hernandez usually comes over on Saturday to collect the Communion host for mass. He comes early, though, because I bake that first thing. He could help you. Sometimes he sends Sister Evangelina and she's no use at all."

Constanza did not elaborate. And Jerry had no idea what "no use" meant from the point of view of a ninety-four-and-a-half-year-old lady who got up at three thirty in the morning seven days a week to bake bread.

Jerry helped Constanza finish cleaning up, and then Constanza began her usual pre-bedtime ritual of laying the wood in the hornos. More words pressed against Jerry's lips, but they would not come out. She wanted to say, "I'll do it myself. I can do it by myself. I've helped you all this week. I know exactly how to lay the wood for the fire. I know which ovens are slow, which fast, in which ones you must pack the wood more densely, which looser. I can do this all by myself, old lady. I want to help you." But none of these words came out.

The moon, a full one, was rising now. The trap-door spiders had finished their nighttime patrols, and the occasional bat swooped through the darkness. Jerry and Constanza laid the wood in the last of the earth ovens. Then, as every night, Constanza gave a mighty yawn and stretched, first putting her hands to the small of her back and then reaching upward and yawning again. Her arms were extremely long, and tonight as she reached her hands into the dusky purple black of the night she seemed to have flattened into a one-dimensional shape, an odd, rangy figure printed against the rising moon. She flicked a hip one way, then the other, to get the cricks out. Next she did a funny little jig to kick the kinks out of her legs. She could have been one of the stick-figure pictures chipped in the sandstone walls of the desert. With her spidery limbs locked in some antic posture, she appeared not quite human but instead some rowdy creature from a long-ago Indian story. Maybe she was the ghost of Kokopelli, the humpbacked flute player.

They walked into the house. "'Night," Constanza

said softly. She had left the flashlight out on the counter if Jerry wanted to look for the sewing machine. It was just past eight, too early to go to bed unless one got up at three thirty in the morning. Jerry did a little bit of homework at the kitchen table, then yawned and went to her bedroom. She stretched out on her bed and began to read the assignment for English class. It was *Romeo and Juliet*. Boy, was the nurse stupid. They were going to have to write a composition on *Romeo and Juliet*. Maybe she would write how if it weren't for the stupid nurse, Romeo and Juliet might have survived. Of course then there would be no tragedy. Maybe Shakespeare could have written it as a comedy. *Romeo, Juliet, and Tubby the Stupid Nurse*. The teacher said they should come up with their own ideas. Her eyes grew heavy. She fell asleep in her clothes on the bed.

There were the little hinges. Silken hinges in her throat, way way in the back. And then the slight muddy taste as the little door started to jiggle. They felt no bigger than grains of sand, but she could feel each one of their eight tiny feet as it crawled up her throat and across her tongue. The hinges squeaked and the trapdoor slammed. Silence.

Jerry woke up, her heart beating wildly. She sat straight up on her bed and slammed her fist against her mouth. It was so real. She couldn't believe it. It had felt so real. She put her other hand to her neck. She closed her eyes and could actually imagine perfectly the trapdoor in the very back of her throat. It had been an awful feeling. She could feel a pulse in her neck throbbing. She got up to get a glass of water. The moon had risen and its light streamed through the window. It was as if she were standing in a silver pool. She was wide awake. There would be no going back to sleep.

Chapter 5

❊

THE CELLAR DOOR creaked as she opened it, and once more Jerry thought of those hinges of silken thread and touched her throat. There were probably zillions of spiders in the cellar. She swung the flashlight around. Its beam was weak. She could almost feel the light leaking out of it. So she pressed the button to flick it off and stood on the cellar steps. And that was when she noticed that the darkness did not look like darkness. It was the color of tea and slightly luminous, as if a flame flickered behind it. Amber-colored tea. The flashlight had made everything a flat, lifeless white, but as Jerry stood there it seemed that this amber air almost began to glow. It must be that this cellar was carved out of the red New Mexican earth. It suddenly struck Jerry that it was very possible that the foundations of

Constanza's house could in fact be the remnants of some sandstone slabs. Maybe one wall had, in another time thousands of years ago, been a cliff. She didn't know much about geology, but she knew that things could shift. Mountains could slide, cliffs tumble; the crust of the earth could even crack open and leave canyons. So where her aunt's house now stood, well, in another time there could have been another landscape, almost another world.

Standing at the top of the steps, she realized that it even smelled like earth and stone. As her eyes adjusted, she could pick out shapes. The shapes seemed to swell up, disembodied like spirits searching for something to attach themselves to and become real objects. She crept down another three steps. Her head bumped softly against a low-hanging lightbulb, but she had no desire to turn it on. Her eyes were sorting things out. She caught her breath as a humpback shape rose in the amber mist of dust and air. But then she almost laughed when she realized it was a bicycle upside-down and askew, sprawled across the top of an ancient bathtub, also upside-down with its claw feet pawing the air. A mouse ran fearlessly across the dirt floor as if it knew exactly what it was doing and where it was going. And near where it had disappeared, Jerry's eyes, now completely accustomed to the dark, spotted a spiderweb. Its filaments looked like sheer gold in the amber light, and a large beetle was snagged and bound in silk in its middle. She stared at the web, transfixed, and wondered where the spider was.

Jerry looked for the sewing machine but not very hard. She was reluctant to poke around too much. It was late besides, and Constanza wouldn't appreciate rattles coming from the cellar at this time of night. But she liked it down here. She liked thinking that this had once been a cliff or the side of a mountain or maybe the bottom of a canyon. She liked the notion that things could shift here—land, shapes, the light itself, and the air. She heard steps overhead in the kitchen. The front door slammed. Surely it couldn't be time for her aunt to start the fires. The moon was up when she had come down, but now a ribbon of pale golden light slipped through a small, high cellar window carved out of the top of one wall.

Jerry climbed the stairs and walked into the kitchen to pour herself a glass of juice. The sun was up. The fires were going. When she looked out the window, she saw a tail of dust whirling up from the road. A car was coming. She watched as Constanza took a pinch of dough from a bowl on a plank. She walked over to the oven she had just raked and threw it in. Jerry watched her curiously.

The car, a battered old station wagon, pulled into the drive. The door opened and an enormous woman in an old-fashioned nun's habit got out. Her wimple lifted in the early morning breeze and her habit billowed out even more. The Sangre de Cristo Mountains behind her were dwarfed. She was, thought Jerry, a mountain range unto herself. "Sister Evangelina here!" She waved jauntily to Jerry, who stood in the doorway of the kitchen. "Here for the host." He won't argue with you, Jerry thought, and grimaced inwardly at her own irreverence. She didn't mean it, of course. This was when it was good not to talk. Suppose something like that had slipped out? "You must be Jerry. Heard all about you from Padre, and of course your aunt."

Constanza was now walking over. "You two meet?"

"After a fashion." Sister Evangelina held out her hand to shake. Jerry took it. It was large and tanned and rough. She remembered the calluses of Father Hernandez's hands.

"Come on in for some coffee," Constanza said.

"Coffee and . . ." Sister Evangelina's voice swooped up.

"Coffee and pastries or whatever I got in there."

"There's a reason I'm this size." She winked. "But it's really not gluttony."

"It better not be a sin if you're eating my baked goods," Constanza said.

"And if it is, we got a lot of sinners in Albuquerque."

Constanza turned to Jerry. "You're up early this morning for a no-school day." Jerry nodded and tried to smile. Constanza glanced at her quickly, and in that split second Jerry knew that her aunt knew she had been in the cellar. They sat at the kitchen table. Constanza brought out a basket of blue-corn muffins and a plate of tartlets similar to the ones she had made earlier in the week.

"You eating these? Or you give them up for Lent?" Constanza began to slide the plate away.

Jerry started as a plump, dark hand darted out and slapped Constanza's. "Stop right there, gal." Jerry's eyes slid toward her aunt.

"Well, if you didn't give up sugar, you must have given up booze," Constanza said cheerfully. Jerry stole a glance at Sister Evangelina.

"Constanza de Luna, what I give up or don't give up for Lent is none of your business." Jerry turned now and looked at her aunt, waiting for the next retort. It was like watching a tennis game. She had never heard so many consecutive sentences coming from her aunt. Suddenly Sister Evangelina threw her brown hands up into the air and hooted. "Mercy, we've shocked the child, Constanza. Bet you've never seen your aunt so crabby or talkative?" When Evangelina laughed, her eyes became little slits above her plump cheeks. "You see, this is one of my gifts. I bring out a different side in people." She fanned her plump fingers in the air.

"Is that why you were called to be a bride of Christ?"

Jerry gasped. "Aunt Constanza!" The words exploded this time, not like before when they slipped out so gently. No, the two words burst off her tongue with a *rat-a-tat-tat*. But this time Aunt Constanza did not tremble. She simply carried on as if nothing special had happened and so did Sister Evangelina.

"Sister Evangelina is used to it," Constanza said.

"Oh, my week wouldn't be complete if I didn't

come over and get insulted by Constanza. She's the only person around who back talks nuns. It reminds me of how relieved I should be that I never had her in a classroom."

"Seeing as I'm twenty years older, that would have been hard."

They sat for a few more minutes, and then Constanza went and got the box with the Communion host for Sister Evangelina. They all walked out to the car together. Sister Evangelina stuffed herself behind the wheel. "Are you coming to the church rummage sale, Constanza?"

"What do I need to do that for?"

"There's bound to be some interesting stuff."

"I don't need any more stuff. I've been collecting stuff for ninety-four years." Jerry bit her lip lightly and thought of the root cellar with its old sandstone walls. Ninety-four years seemed like nothing compared to rock time. But it was as if time stopped down there, or was suspended, or maybe just didn't count for much. Something happened down there. She thought of the mouse. Did it ever come up into the daylight? Or the spider, the invisible spider. If she went back, would the beetle be gone? Eaten? Not escaped. She felt certain that nothing really escaped from the root cellar.

"Well, then it's time to get rid of some stuff."

Constanza scuffed the toe of her boot in the dirt. "Naw, I don't think so."

"You should see the two of you," Sister Evangelina said suddenly. "Both of you scratching your heads exactly the same way. Constanza, Jerry's been here barely a week and is already picking up your bad habits."

"Well, maybe I should send her over to you and she'll get some of your bad habits and pork up."

Aunt! The word rumbled Jerry's head but remained silent.

"Oh my word!" hooted Sister Evangelina. She started the car and began to back out. There was a screeching sound.

"Damn. She's going to grind those gears out. Nuns are the lousiest drivers."

"I know what you're saying, Constanza," Sister Evangelina yelled from the car. "'Nuns are lousy drivers.' Well, as little Miguel Guiterro said to Sister Clara the other day, 'Up yours.'" She waved gaily out the window as she drove down the driveway.

Chapter 6

❧

"MAYBE YOUR FRIEND will help you get that sewing machine up from the cellar," Constanza said when Sinta came over later that afternoon.

"You got a sewing machine here?" Sinta said.

Jerry shrugged and smiled. She wished the words would come again with Sinta.

"Yes," Constanza said. "I was telling Jerry, though, that it is an old one. Not electric, just a treadle that you pump."

"Let's get it," Sinta said.

Jerry didn't know what to do. She did not want to go back to the cellar with anybody. It was as if someone else might break its spell. The amber would bleed out of the light. Bicycles would look just like bicycles and tubs like tubs. "Come on." Sinta gave her shoulder a tap.

They went down into the cellar with Jerry carrying the flashlight. "Lot of stuff down here," Sinta said as they reached the last step. "Guess by the time you're as old as your aunt, you've accumulated a lot."

Jerry found the sewing machine immediately. She beckoned with her flashlight.

"Here it is!" Sinta said. "Oh, look, it's absolutely coated in dust. We should clean it off before we take it upstairs."

Jerry panicked. She already thought of the cellar as her place. "No!" The word popped out.

Sinta looked up. "Jerry, you spoke." Jerry nodded. Her mouth tried to move around a few words, but no sound came. "One? Two? Is that what you're saying?" Sinta asked. Jerry nodded. "One or two words, is that what you mean? You've spoken a few words?" Jerry nodded again and walked over to where Sinta stood by the machine. It wasn't that heavy.

Just before they left the cellar, Jerry turned to look for the spiderweb. It was still there. It looked quite ordinary now, but the beetle was gone.

Jerry and Sinta took the sewing machine upstairs and directly into the cook yard. Jerry went to get some dust cloths.

"I think we're going to need some oil," Sinta said when Jerry came back. "The wheel is sort of stiff."

A half hour later the machine was cleaned and oiled. They had just begun to thread it. Jerry reached for the pieces of the skirt that she had cut out. She had already pinned them together. They were ready to stitch. She slipped the two pieces in. "I wish I had done a straight skirt instead of a blouse. It would be so much simpler," Sinta said.

Jerry began to pump the treadle. The needle dropped down into the cloth. She gently pushed the cloth on the small plate under the foot that clamped the needle. "Oh, look what a nice stitch." Sinta spoke softly. "And you can go just at your own speed. This is so much easier."

The weather was warm and they had actually set up the sewing machine on the porch that stretched across the back of the house. Instead of a railing at the edge, there was a low adobe wall on which Constanza had set scores of flowerpots. Some grew herbs; some dropped silvery green vines over the edge that hung like lace; some had bright red geraniums. On top of the wall and in niches were Constanza's souvenirs that had either somehow mysteriously arrived in her yard or she had picked up while traveling about delivering bread. There was an iron piece that looked like a fish skeleton, but Jerry thought might be a long-handled cooking instrument for use in a fire. There was part of a cow's skull and the bones from what looked like a bird's wing that Constanza had arranged in a pretty design. There was also a little terra-cotta figure of the Virgin Mary. There were in fact many of the small wooden carved figures of saints called *bultos*.

Jerry had nearly finished the seams on her skirt and Sinta was trying to set in the sleeve on one side of her blouse. "I wish I could get this sleeve to not puff up so much at the shoulder. I don't want to look like a football player."

Just at that moment Constanza came out with a pitcher of lemonade and some pine-nut cookies fresh from the range. She set down the tray. "Let me look at it," she said, holding out her hands for the blouse Sinta was working on. She spread it out on the table and unpinned the sleeve. "Will you let me make a few little slits in the edges here where the sleeve joins the shoulder hole? That will make it set better."

"Sure," said Sinta.

The long, knobby fingers began to snip and pin.

"It's just like crimping a pie crust," Constanza said, and handed it back to Sinta.

"Oh, thank you so much." Sinta paused. "I asked Jerry if she wanted to go to the movies with me tonight, but I don't think she wants to." Jerry looked down at her sewing.

"Well, it's up to Jerry," Constanza said. "Maybe some other time."

Sinta began gathering up her things as her mother had just pulled up in her car. Jerry and Constanza walked with her toward the drive. Sinta turned to wave as she climbed into the car. Jerry waved back absently. She was thinking about the cellar. When she had turned to look around just before she and Sinta came up, she had thought it looked ordinary. But she knew it wasn't. She knew if she went down again, it wouldn't seem ordinary at all.

Chapter 7

❖❖❖

JERRY HELPED CONSTANZA in the cook yard for the rest of the afternoon. Then Constanza came over as Jerry was raking out the last oven. She was holding a bunch of scraggly-looking roots.

"Seed onions," Constanza said. "Ugly, aren't they?" She snorted and held up the bunch. When she held them that way, with their white, dry roots pulled back, the onions did look a bit like bony heads with scraggly hair. "Want to help me plant them? I always plant my onions in early March, then put cold frames upside down on them. It's warm now, but you never know when a blizzard can sweep down from the mountains."

Jerry nodded.

"Good! I'll get the rototiller. Teach you how to drive it."

Jerry wondered if this was something she had to ride like a tractor. Constanza returned a few minutes later pushing a machine about the size of a small lawn mower.

She pulled the starter cord and the motor roared. Then Constanza immediately turned it off. "Now you try." Jerry looked at her. "Go on. This is something you got to learn how to do. Start an engine with a whipcord."

Jerry bent down and pulled on the cord. She heard a small wheeze of a wheel turning. "You got to snap it smart like. It's all in the snap." Jerry tried two more times. She got it to sputter. "See, it's harder than starting a car. I think cars should have whipcords—make them more challenging. Harder for robbers to get away too."

On the fourth try Jerry got it.

"Okay, now I'm going to throw it into gear. Hang on."

Jesus! Jerry thought. The thing leaped out in front of her and took on a life of its own. She hung on. The vibrations were huge. She felt her arms might shiver out of her shoulder sockets.

Constanza was yelling at her over the roar. "Head for that patch right in front of you." Jerry jiggered over to where Constanza was pointing, her teeth rattling, her hair quivering. Even her eyeballs seemed to shake. "Now tip it forward so it can lock into the dirt." The rotary blades sliced through the soil. "Don't worry about keeping it straight, just try to keep a steady pressure on it."

Jerry watched as the red soil came up in little clumps. "Good job. Now turn the corner. Just tip it back a little bit. There you go."

Twenty minutes later the onion patch was tilled. Constanza gave her a trowel, and together Jerry and her aunt sank down on their knees and began to dig holes for the seed onions. The soil was soft and damp, and Jerry could almost feel it drink up the last of the vibrations that still ricocheted through her body. The earth smelled like the root cellar. She could almost imagine that glow behind the light that seemed to saturate the air.

After they had finished planting the onions, she helped her aunt arrange the cold frames on top.

"Oh, look," said Constanza. "That glass pane over in the corner of this frame is half in, half out. I'm going to have to reset it with some putty. Tell you what, Jerry, go down to the root cellar. There's a can of putty on the shelf just beneath the window.

Fetch it for me. I don't think I'll do it today, it's getting late. But if you can put the can by the sink in the kitchen, I'll remember to do it tomorrow."

Jerry opened the cellar door. The dim amber light seemed to reach out for her. As she walked down the stairs, she felt as if with each step she was melting through the curtains of amber light. She found the putty can. But she didn't want to leave. She touched the walls. They were sandstone. When she looked at her fingertips, there were minute particles that left on her skin a reddish tinge. Did she hear something in a corner to her right? Was it the mouse? Certainly she could never hear a spider, not even down here where the silence was so thick. But it seemed as if something furtive and hidden was happening. She turned toward the corner where she thought the noise might have come from. The window behind her let in the last of the day's light and illuminated a trunk with a high, curved top. It stood behind the veils of amber light, apart and aloof and with a muffled gleam, faint like the glow of a guttering flame. Yet it seemed to almost dare Jerry to come closer. She took one hesitant step and then another. There was silence, complete and perfect silence. Flawless, indestructible silence. But then Jerry felt a cold chill and the hair on the back of her neck stood up. Children's voices. Faint laughter melted out of the amber light. She turned and tore up the stairs.

Jerry knew she would have to go back.

Chapter 8

❧❦❧

JERRY WAITED UNTIL midnight, when her aunt would be asleep. Then she crept out of bed. She looked out the kitchen window. Everything was so quiet, so still. The entire land seemed wrapped in silence. She was not frightened. She went down the stairs, her eyes adjusting to the darkness that was not really darkness. She was not really surprised when she finally saw the fat spider suspended on a silken thread just by the trunk. It was as if the spider had been waiting for her and decided to spin another web just to have something to do while waiting.

Jerry ran her fingertips lightly over the top of the trunk. A shiver ran through her. Her fingers seemed electrified. She swept them across again. Did she feel a design in the top? She bent her face closer and noticed that there was a pattern of little pinpricks. It was as if her finger-tips had been dusted with iron filings and the pin-pricks were the magnets drawing them to the trunk. These were letters she was touching. She could deduce their shape. The first was an *s*. She could feel the opposing curves that made the letter. The next was much smaller, a *d* possibly, and then a straight vertical line. At the bottom it met with another at a right angle. An *l*! So the initials must be SdL.

She lifted the latch. This time it was not silent, and the creak startled her. But the latch simply fell off into her hand. How long had it been since any-one had opened this trunk? Had Constanza lived ninety-four years and never opened it? Did this con-stitute some sort of trespassing? Jerry wondered. As she lifted its lid, she realized that this was beyond right or wrong.

A veil of dust drifted down from the interior of the lid. The contents seemed neatly arranged, although Jerry could not tell at first exactly what they were. Some were shallow boxes; some things were wrapped in ancient-looking tissue paper, some in Spanish newspapers. There were odd bits of fab-ric, a picture frame with no picture, a Bible, a cup tarnished nearly black with age, something that looked like a corncob with a bit of worn fabric wrapped around its middle. Nothing too unusual at first glance. And yet all strangely compelling. Who did this stuff belong to, these bits and pieces? She sensed that she had at her fingertips the fragments of a puzzle. An extraordinary kind of three-dimensional jigsaw puzzle, a puzzle of time and space. The cup had been wrapped in newspaper, but there was no date on the paper. The printing, however, looked odd. She sensed that it had come from a time even before her Aunt Constanza had been born. When she set the cup back, she noticed the corner of what appeared to be some lace. She dared not pull on it. Yellow with age, the lace seemed as if it might turn to dust with the slightest touch. Carefully she lifted the Bible and the empty picture frame that lay on top of the lace. Jerry stared at the lace. It was folded over and appeared somewhat larger than a handkerchief. There was a dull stain toward the center of it.

She felt her heart begin to beat harder and she lifted her hand to the crown of her head and began to rub her hair. There was something terribly disconcerting about this lace. It was connected with those faint voices she had heard, the dim voices of children. A chill crept up the very bones of her fingers, but still she reached into the trunk and picked up the piece of lace. Jerry lifted the lace close to her face to see it better. It had a pleasant woody smell, like piñon or perhaps cedar. She held the lace and studied its design. There was a pattern, beautiful and delicate. Time began to bend. She closed her eyes. She saw flickerings on the inside of her eyelids, a crazy jig of little particles and squiggly lines. There had been another girl who had rubbed her head in just the same way as Jerry. Maybe she had even stuffed this piece of lace into her mouth to muffle a shriek, a cry. Maybe she had bitten the lace as Jerry had bitten a sleeping bag—to make it all silent. But this long-ago girl was not Aunt Constanza. It was another little girl in another place, another country, another time. . . .

In the House of the Lace Maker
STREET OF THE LITTLE PEPPERS
SEVILLE, SPAIN
JUNE 1391

❧❧❧

Miriam

"Reyna! Reyna!"

I hear Mama yelling for my sister. She must be

too close to the gates of the Jewish Quarter. Mama is always afraid that we are going to go outside the gates. She spends half her day calling for us. It has been forbidden for Jews to leave the quarter since the terrible days in March. It is the bad friar Martinez. He makes decrees. He orders conversions of Jews. He makes rules about what we can do and where we can go and what businesses we can have. Sometimes I think he is more powerful than the king and queen. Don Solomon, our good friend, believes this. He says the friar does not need the king and queen. He needs only the little people, the *pueblo menudo*, because between his genius and their ignorance he has created a monster of evil for Jews. He whips those little people into a frenzy against us. It is a scary time. A time of great danger. And that is why Mama spends her days calling for us. She does not want us out of her sight, much less outside the quarter.

"Miriam!" Mama calls upstairs. "Go get your sister. It's almost time to light the candles for Sabbath. The sun is going down. Everything must be ready." Then she tries to add gaily, "The Sabbath bride comes."

That's what Mama calls Friday evenings when we have our special dinner—she calls it the

Sabbath bride, for everything is pretty and clean and a special white tablecloth is laid on our table.

"Miriam!" She calls again.

I find Reyna. She is by the gates with a group of girls. They are actually joking with a guard on the other side. Mama would be furious. "Come on, Reyna, Mama needs your help. It's nearly time for the . . ." But I don't say it. I don't want to talk about Jewish things in front of a guard who is paid to keep us in. Reyna and I walk back in the dusky light. We wind through the narrow streets of the quarter. Most of the shops are already shuttered for the Sabbath. I can smell good smells—chicken with olives, sometimes lamb with cinnamon. Shadows fall across us and I feel a chill. Reyna throws her big shawl over the two of us. "I wonder," she says, "if things will ever be normal again."

I wonder if I shall even remember what normal is.

We slip in the door just in time. Mama already has her prettiest ivory lace shawl over her head. She looks like a bride from behind as she stands in front of the table that is against the wall. We slide in beside her. She lights the two candles and now raises her hands, covering her eyes as she recites the blessing. When she is finished, she turns and kisses each of us. My poor mama. She does not exactly look like a young bride. Her face has grown more lines—more come each day—and her hair is turning white.

I am too young to have a white-haired mama. I am too young to have a dead father. Mama and Reyna go out to the kitchen to help the maid, Annuncia, with the rest of the preparations for dinner. Mama gives me some small task to keep me away, but I can hear them talking in whispery voices. I am not supposed to hear. But I know what they are talking about—the friar Martinez. They say he is getting worse. I don't know. I just know that I do not like to think about it. I especially do not like to think about my friend Ruta. She converted. They took her to a church. They sprinkled water on her head, and I think it only gave her a big head. Yes, that is what I think. She is so stuck-up now. Always showing off how she's learned some things she calls the *Credo* and the *Ave*. She said that when Friar Martinez rushed into the synagogue in Córdoba, where her aunt lives, crosses appeared in the air. They hung there for just a minute in the sunlight coming through the windows.

Her name is no longer Ruta. It is Immaculata.

When she was baptized, they gave her a Christian name. Imagine me calling her that! Such a long silly name after being called Ruta. I forget all the time and she gets very snippy about it. So I call her nothing most of the time. If I see her in the alley and maybe want to play sticks and pebbles, I just say, *"Oiga!"* "Hey, hey you." I know it's rude. I don't care.

Anyway, I am not thinking of any of this, for tonight Solomon Ben Asher comes to our house for dinner. When Don Solomon comes, it makes the Sabbath even more special. He always has sweets and ribbons in his pockets. Sweets for me and ribbons for Reyna, who now that she is fourteen wears her hair up. Don Solomon is a physician and an astronomer to the court of King Enrique and Queen Catarina. Don Solomon was here when Papa's heart stopped after the riots in March, when the mobs stormed into the Jewish Quarter. They did not come up our street, but they got to Papa's warehouse on the Street of the Grapes. They broke all the casks and the sherry flowed across the cobblestones and filled the gutters. Mama says it was a blessing that it was simply his heart that stopped, not like Señor Perera. Something terrible happened to him. I have heard whispers. But what is so simple about a heart stopping to beat? Now Papa is dead.

I hear a rap at the door. It must be Don Solomon. Annuncia goes to answer it. "Ah, Doña Grazia," he greets Mama. He is dressed in his court clothes, a *sayo*, a kind of sleeveless jerkin made of brocaded cloth that is belted at the waist. Underneath he wears a silk shirt with billowing sleeves. On his head there is a tall scarlet hat, which signifies that he is a Jewish physician. He looks very handsome and very dignified, I think. But best of all his hat has gold braid, which means he serves in the court of the king and queen.

It is my job to take Don Solomon's hat when he arrives. So I always try to stand as tall as I can, even though I am short for my ten years. After he has bowed to my mother and my sister, he turns to me. "Señorita Miriam," and with a flourish he takes off his hat and gives it to me. This is the best thing about his hat: It smells like limes. Reyna says it is an oil that he uses on his hair. And even though Don Solomon is slightly roly-poly, I believe he is a most elegant man. When I take his hat, he makes me feel elegant too. So I always dip my knees slightly in a curtsy, and each time Don Solomon murmurs the words *"Adecuado por la corte."* This means that I am suitable for the court of the king and queen. He says this so softly, though. I wish he would say the words a little louder so I can be sure Mama and Reyna hear. Next he reaches into his pocket for his green velvet cap and something always falls out. With a flash of his hand he catches it. Or sometimes he puts the green cap on his head and something dangles from the edge. Then looking up he will comically cross his eyes. "What have we here? Aah! A sweet?" And he whisks a twist of brown paper from his hat and gives it to me. Rolled inside is a honey stick or maybe my very favorite, a violet crinkle all sparkly with sugar crystals. For Reyna there is a velvet ribbon or sometimes a braid pin or a small vial of perfume. And I dip another curtsy.

But tonight there is a difference. I felt it from my first curtsy. First Don Solomon did not speak the words *"Adecuado por la corte."* And I know I did the curtsy perfectly. His manner was exceedingly grave and he nearly forgot to give me the candy. Then through dinner they seem to talk of only the most boring things. I look down and concentrate on my plate. I press my spoon into the rice to make a little lake for the rich beef broth.

After Annuncia clears the bowls, she brings in a plate of figs and grapes.

"So how goes the piece for the archbishop?"

"Oh, I am just doing the sleeve trim lace now. The sisters at the convent will do the hem."

"That's because the sleeve lace must float, and everyone knows Mama's lace is the most filmy," Reyna interjected.

"Don't brag, Reyna. I wouldn't have time to do the hem. The sisters do a very fine job."

"Ah, show it to me," Don Solomon said. "You know how I love to see your work."

This is a game that Don Solomon and Mama play. Mama shows him a piece of lace, and he guesses what gave her the idea for the pattern. They rise to leave the table and go to the front room. By the largest window there is a chair with a stand and on the stand a dark pillow. Pinned to the pillow is a gossamer web of lace, and radiating from its edges are the fine silk threads tied to dozens of bobbins made from bone.

"My good woman, how many bobbins are you working with on this one?"

"Oh, forty pair," Doña Grazia replied. "It's a very complicated design."

Don Solomon holds a candle close to the pillow. "Let me see now if I can guess that design." Don Solomon scratches his chin, then adjusts his velvet cap. His brow furrows.

"You'll never guess," I say. "And I am the one who found it!"

"Found what?" Don Solomon asks.

"The thing that gave Mama the idea. But I can't tell you until you guess."

"A spiderweb."

"No, Don Solomon. Every time you guess a spiderweb."

"But my dear Miriam, do you know how many different kinds of spiders there are and how many different kind of webs they weave? And do you know what the best spiderweb is for dressing a wound and stanching the bleeding?"

"No," Reyna and I both say at once.

"An orb weaver's web. The silk is the best. Only laudable pus follows, nothing fetid. It is the best way to dress a wound or ulcers. Such a creature should be celebrated in lace."

"But it is not a spider's web, Don Solomon," I say,

pointing at the lace on the pillow. "Come on now, take another guess."

He thinks another moment, scratches his chin again. "Ah!" he says, lifting one finger. "The veins of a butterfly's wings."

Mama laughs. "Miriam, run get your inspiration."

I go to the cupboard and take out a small box and open it. "See!" Don Solomon squints into the box. An insect with translucent wings lies dead on a piece of cotton. "A dragonfly."

"Yes." Mama nods. "Miriam found this one dead, floating on the water of the cistern in the square."

"But look, Don Solomon," I say. "Look at the little designs. They are like tiny tiles but clear as glass. Look at their pattern. Are they not the most beautiful? And you see the shapes are not all the same. They all differ just a tiny bit and nothing too perfect, too sharp or square."

Don Solomon stands back and looks at me with deep, penetrating eyes. "You should become a student of geometry."

"What is geometry?"

"Why, it is the study and measurement of the shapes of things. There are laws, rules that when applied to points and lines and planes help one calculate the dimensions of space. One can map a dragonfly's wing or perhaps the world using geometry."

"Oh, I want to learn! Please."

"Don Solomon." Mama raises her finger. "Please don't put any more ideas into this child's head. She's already making a nuisance about learning how to read."

"But I want to," I whine.

"We have enough troubles in the quarter without little Jewish girls learning to read. That's all that crazy Friar Martinez needs to hear, that we are teaching girls in the quarter to read." Mama quickly clamps her mouth shut. She had not meant to speak of the friar or any of the troubles. But now I know I am going to be sent to bed so they can speak of such things. They can't wait to get me off to bed. But what they don't know is that I shall still hear them. Yes, in my bedroom on the second floor there is an air vent. This vent not only brings up the warmth from the fire in the winter and the cooler air in the summer, but their voices as well. With my ear pressed to this hole, I can hear everything!

"I think, Doña Grazia . . ." There was a pause. "No, pardon me, I *know* that you and your daughters must leave Seville immediately." I almost gasp and press my ear closer to the grate of the vent.

"What? Leave Seville?"

"It is no longer safe."

"But the walls of the Jewish Quarter here are guarded. It won't be like in March."

"You are right. It will be worse."

"Worse? How can it be worse?" Mama says in a voice so low I can barely hear her.

"They will burn the gates."

"But did you not talk with the archbishop? The archbishop is sympathetic, no?"

"Of course he is sympathetic. The king is sympathetic. He has a court full of Jews—Jews like me, physicians and scientists. His best tax farmers are Jews, his chief accountant is a Jew, as is the secretary to the king."

"So why can't he and the archbishop stop it?" Mama hisses in frustration.

"Why? Because what is happening is the work of the mobs, the lowest classes. That is Martinez's genius. How he rouses them! Now tonight they are demanding the police chief's removal because he jailed that rabble who tried to burn the synagogue, and it is said that even the nobles are split on this.

You must leave tomorrow."

"Where? Where does a widow with two daughters go?"

"Toledo. You have family in Toledo."

"Will Toledo be any better? What if this spreads?"

"It won't spread that fast. Just get out, Doña Grazia. I can arrange a wagon. I shall come in the morning."

I cannot believe what I am hearing. Mama is right—where would we go? It is exciting but scary. Suddenly I hear something, louder than Mama's voice or Don Solomon's. At first I thought it was a wind, the cold north one that sweeps down in winter from the Sierra Nevada. But it is hot now and this wind comes with shrieks and shouts. I start to shake. I cover my ears. Horrible, horrible words like needles in my ears. I press harder with my hands. *"Muerte a los Matadors de Christo."* "Death to the Christ Killers."

There is a terrible crushing sound and a storm of feet in the street. Then the smell of burning wood. The gates of the quarter must be on fire! This cannot be happening. I think that somehow I can make this unhappen. I feel the violet crinkle in my pocket.

"Here," I say to myself, "I am going to make a little bargain." I slip the violet crinkle into my mouth and clamp my hands over my ears. This is the bargain: If I can keep the sound from my ears and the sweetness in my mouth, Mama, Reyna, Don Solomon, and I shall all live. But now there is a terrible scream, like flames in my head it roars. My hands fall from my ears. The violet sugar seeps from the corner of my mouth. I am losing this bargain.

No hay cruces. There are no crosses hanging in the air as Ruta said there were in Córdoba, but here I am in the church of Santa Catalina de la Blanca. There is blood on my dress and a streak of blood on Mama's face. It is the blood of Don Solomon. Reyna too wears his blood. The mobs have taken us. We rode them like a wave to the church. We did not walk, no. We were seized and then told at sword point to march. "*Agua o espada,*" water or sword. We had then no idea what they were talking about. Mendez the apothecary, his wife, and two little ones rode the wave as well. And then there was the old man who sells pomegranates on the Street of the Levies, Señor Piñero. He died before they got him to the church. One of the mob snatched the lace from Mama's stand. I thought she was taking it for herself, but this is strange; she is now coming up to me with the lace. She is babbling sweetly to me. It is almost baby talk. This same woman who kicked Don Solomon in the face as he lay dying on the floor of our house is now murmuring to me as if I am the most adorable child. She pinches my cheeks softly and coos at me. "*La muchacha linda . . . pequeña querida. . . . Pequeña dulce . . .* pretty girl . . . little cutie, little dear one, little sweetie." Yes, little sweetie with violet sugar crinkles and blood on her face. The woman is taking the piece of lace that Mama made for the archbishop's sleeve. It too has blood on it. She is placing it on my head and she is leading me to the altar.

A man with a smile like a thin blade speaks. "*Niña, Bievenida a la fe verdadera. . . .*" "Child, Welcome to the true faith." I know who this man is, even though I have never seen him before. I know it is the friar, Friar Martinez. His eyes are pale brown, almost yellow. His skin bloodless. The yellow eyes peer at me over the beak of a nose as if he is looking at an insect. But there is something coiled within him like a snake. It is pure hatred. I see it.

The woman placed the lace on my head and now

he removes it and the woman puts it on my shoulders and he begins to mumble some words in a language I do not understand. There is a stone bowl of water on a pedestal. He waves his hands over it and then he pours some oil on his fingers. He presses his oily thumb to my head and my chin and then on each cheek. All the while he is muttering in the strange language. The woman hisses in my ear that each time she pokes me I am to say *"sí"*—"yes" to the friar's questions. So I do. I feel her finger in my side, but I can see my mother. Her face is the color of the stone bowl. Reyna's eyes are wide and fixed. It is like a death stare. He pours a cup of water on my head. He sprinkles some on the white lace around my shoulders, and finally he gives me a candle. I don't know what to do with it. Then he says in Spanish, *"Maria. Su nombre esta Maria ahorra. Uno buen nombre Cristiano . . . nombrado de la virgen bendecida Maria."* "Your name is Maria now. A good Christian name . . . the name of the Blessed Virgin Mary."

And now it has been four hours since I was baptized in the church and Reyna and Mama as well. We had no choice. *Agua o espada*. Now we know the meaning. "The holy water or the sword." The streets run with the blood of those who did not choose the water. Mama now takes that same piece of lace that I wore and she scrubs the tops of our heads. I want to cry. "No, Mama." She scrubs so hard it burns. I shall have no hair left there. She does the same to Reyna. And then herself. Finally she throws the lace, which is tattered now, into a corner. The lace that has Don Solomon's blood. Tomorrow, she says, we shall go to Toledo. There is nothing left for us here.

This is the last night we shall ever spend in our house. Everyone is asleep now. But I cannot sleep, so I have come downstairs just to sit, I guess. There is this deathly quiet that lies across the quarter as thickly as the smoke from the gates that still smolder. I think I came downstairs really to see the place where Don Solomon had lain dead. Mama would be so angry if she knew I was down here. Or maybe she wouldn't. Does anything really matter anymore?

I cannot taste violet crinkles in my mouth. I cannot even remember their taste on my tongue. I feel a warm, sick feeling rising in the back of my throat. I swallow hard and feel my forehead turn hot. There is no holding this in. And now I stand in my own vomit in the very place on the floor where Don Solomon died. Not five hours ago.

I'll go sit in the chair by the window. In the distance I can hear the town crier. He is calling for Jews, any Jews still alive, to come immediately to the church. There will be another group baptism. Suddenly my eye catches the piece of lace Mama had thrown away in disgust after our baptism. I'm going to keep it. I don't know why, but I need to keep this scrap of lace stained with the blood of Don Solomon. I find a strand of my hair is still entwined in the threads. Maybe this will always connect me with Don Solomon in some way. My head still burns where Mama rubbed it with this lace. I keep touching the place on my head. I can't get rid of the burning feeling. I am going to keep this lace forever and ever. I swear it.

I will never forget this night of holy water and blood and vomit and oil and the friar with a smile like a knife's blade. Just because they call me Maria does not make me Maria. And I'm not just a New Christian because they told me so. No. Not at all. No, you know what I have become? An old woman. Can't get rid of that burning feeling on top of my head. From the window by Mama's lace-making stand I can see a star rise over a rooftop. This morning I was ten years old. Tonight I am older than the stars.

Chapter 9

❖❖❖

JERRY PRESSED HER hands against her eyes as she climbed the stairs out of the cellar and into the frail light of the dawn kitchen. She would come out into this new morning and everything would somehow make sense. She wasn't sure what had happened down there. But it certainly didn't make sense, and there was no room for nonsense in her world. Silence defined the world of Jerry Luna. This had to have been a dream. If it were a dream, it would not scare her, not really. She would just consign it to that place of scary dreams. And this was definitely a scary dream. That was all. But she had no desire to explain it.

She closed the door to the cellar firmly behind her. She even pressed her fingers along the edges as if to seal the crack between the door and the frame. She knew it was stupid.

But those things that she had heard needed to be buried. They needed to remain down there. She was up here. Up here in her aunt's kitchen. The can of putty that she had brought up for her aunt the previous day, when she had last gone to the cellar, stood accusingly on the counter. How could she have forgotten to take it back down after her aunt had used it! Well, tough. She wasn't going back down for a stupid can of putty. Let Constanza do it. She walked over to the kitchen sink and washed her hands. Her fingers had a light film of dust. She held them under the faucet, watching the amber swirl down the drain. But she had left streaks on the bar of soap. So she rinsed that and then her hands once more. There, it was all gone.

She glanced at the clock on the wall. Nearly five o'clock. She would take a shower and get dressed. She would go out in the cook yard and help Aunt Constanza. She would try to say words. Yes, she was going to be normal. In the shower Jerry scrubbed herself hard. She wanted none of that amber dust clinging to her. And she tried to practice saying the few words she had spoken. *I hope they never get into your bread*. And she had gasped *Aunt Constanza* when her aunt had said that shocking thing to

Sister Evangelina. But the words wouldn't come out. Her throat began having that funny weak feeling again. She felt a blackness rise in her stomach as if she had just been punched hard in the gut. It felt like dread, and it rose and spread slowly like a shadow in her mind: The words were creeping back down into the cellar, through a trapdoor. They were her words, but they were separate from her. They would take on a life of their own—down there. It was a devastating thought.

Jerry crouched on the shower floor and let the hot water beat down on her. *I'm mute. I'm not crazy. I'm mute I'm not crazy.* She repeated these words in her head over and over to the rhythm of the beating water. They roiled in her head like a chant, nearly breaking up in meaning and becoming a kind of senseless song: *I'm mute. I'm not crazy I'm mute not crazy mute not crazy mute not crazy older than the stars not crazy older than the stars mute stars not crazy stars . . .*

But Jerry did not even realize what she was silently saying when the stars slipped into song. She did not even know that some of the words she chanted were spoken by the other girl in another place, in another country, in another time, more than six hundred years ago.

By the time Jerry dressed and went into the cook yard, she felt good, in control, calm, and most important, normal. It *had* been a dream. She knew this. It would dissolve like the dust particles in the stream of sink water. It had already swirled away. She picked up one of the long-handled wooden pallets and began to slide the round loaves into the ovens.

"Thank you, Jerry. My, you're up early again," Aunt Constanza said, her head half in a dead oven that she was repairing with something she called "Aunt Constanza's mixit up stickit up fixit up," which she claimed had the hair of a prairie dog mixed with cactus juice and dried cow patties, and was perfect for sealing cracks in a horno.

The next morning, Monday, Jerry was early for school. She went to her homeroom and began to work on her English assignment. It was not due for a week. They were supposed to select their favorite passage from *Romeo and Juliet* and explain why they loved it. There was a passage she kind of remembered. It was in act three after Tybalt has been killed by Romeo, and Juliet finds out that Romeo has been banished and she is all torn up. She is even imagining what would happen if he were to die. Poor Juliet. "What to do? What to do?" The words bounced around silently in Jerry's head as she flicked the pages of the play searching for the passage. Too bad she couldn't get hold of the Cliffs Notes. But Miss Lafferty flunked anyone caught with Cliffs Notes. Ah, there it was, scene two. Jerry began to read the words. And although she did not realize it, her lips tried to move around the lovely shapes. "For thou wilt lie upon the wings of night, / Whiter than new snow upon a raven's back. / Come gentle night, / Come, loving, black-brow'd night, / Give me my Romeo, and, when he shall die / Take him and cut him out in little stars / And he will make the face of heaven so fine / That all the world will be in love with the night, / And pay no worship to the garish sun."

The meter flowed into her senses and into the very core of her mind. And then she stopped. She could not read it, nor copy it. She did not want to think of the stars, those stars older than Juliet, and Juliet soon to be older than the stars. Jerry clamped her eyes shut and flipped quickly back through the pages. She made a deal with herself—whatever page she turned to, she would look at, point her finger, take the quote closest to her finger, and write about it.

Oh my God, she muttered silently as her finger stopped in the middle of the left-hand page of act one, scene five. *That stupid over-the-top speech by Romeo.* She took her pen and began copying it down: "O! she doth teach the torches to burn bright. / It seems she hangs upon the cheek of night." *Cheek of night, give me a friggin' break!* "Like a rich jewel in an Ethiop's ear;" *"Whoever she is! Ethiop, what the hell is an Ethiop? Person from Ethiopia?"* "Beauty too rich for use, for earth too dear! / So shows a snowy dove trooping with crows, / As yonder lady o'er her fellows shows. / The measure done, I'll watch her place of stand, / And, touching hers, make blessed my rude hand. *"Buck up, Romeo, quit groveling. Nothing wrong with your hands. Oh my God, what a googly-eyed wimp. Spare me!*

Well, she would write something about this. Miss Lafferty said it only had to be three hundred words. At least there were no stars in this one. Three hundred words, did that include the words in quotation or not?

Chapter 10

❖❖❖❖

ONCE AGAIN IT WAS Friday night, and once again as Jerry came out of her room she saw the back of her aunt as she stood in front of the window lighting her Lenten candles. The window itself was a rectangle of lavender light, with her aunt's face mirrored in the glass. And just beneath her eyes, which were shut tight in some sort of prayer, there were the reflections of the flickering candle flames. A bolt of lightning popped across the sky, jagged and hot white, slicing the window on the diagonal, splitting the image of her aunt's face.

Thunder rumbled as they sat down to their dinner, and outside the sky flinched with lightning that spread like electric lace over the mountains.

"You want a little wine, Jerry? You can have

some. It won't kill you. And it's a heck of a lot better than that stuff they give us at Communion. Friday night, you know."

Jerry shrugged. She really meant to say no. She tried to make her mouth move around the simple word, but ever since . . . well, she didn't want to think about "ever since." Even so, she stole a glance at the cellar door, then slid her eyes to where the putty can had been. It was still there.

"Nnnah." The chopped sound came out with a mighty effort. It felt as if she were spitting a chunk of rock.

"I'll take that for a 'no,'" Constanza said softly, and then quite suddenly reached over and patted Jerry's hand. "It's fine, gal. You're doing just fine."

Jerry felt an unfamiliar sting in her eyes. Was she going to actually cry? She did not want to cry. Constanza got up quickly from the table. "Forgot the raisins. This stew always tastes better with raisins."

Jerry could see that there were already raisins in the stew. Constanza had not forgotten them at all. Her aunt was not a good liar, but her intentions were good.

She came back to the table with the box and sprinkled some on top.

"A garnish, you know. Just for decoration, really," Constanza explained, and then they began to eat, both pretending about the raisins—about the raisins being just a garnish.

Later, after dinner, after they had gone out to look for trapdoor spiders, after the dishes were cleaned and dried and put away on the pine shelves, and after Constanza had gone to bed and Jerry had stuck on nearly one hundred "Constanza Delivers" labels to the baked-goods boxes in the back pantry, a task she knew Constanza loathed, and after she had lain in bed for almost two hours staring at the ceiling unable to sleep, Jerry began to think about the silent lies she had told in the past two days—the two days since "the ever since." Yes, she reflected on how one did not have to speak to be a liar. She had written a very excellent, exactly three-hundred-word essay (excluding the quote) about why Romeo's stupid speech moved her profoundly. She had just agreed that there were no raisins in the stew. Let's see, what else? she mused. Oh, Jerry's silent voices could be very sarcastic and cutting. Perhaps that was why her voice had deserted her, because her tongue was gnarled with lies. She squeezed her eyes shut as she remembered the touch of her aunt's hand on her own.

Then she suddenly got up. She knew what she had to do. It was time to think of "the ever since." She refused to be pinned in by "the ever since" and the silent lies. So she walked out of her bedroom, down the hall, and to the kitchen. It was a moonless night, a night of deep shadows. She could barely discern the outline of the cellar door, and yet she moved inexorably toward it. She opened the door and stood on the first step. She let her eyes adjust and then began to descend the stairs. Her steps were sure, her vision clear, but her heart beat madly as she lifted the lid of the trunk.

The lace was exactly where she had left it. She picked it up, looked at it, and replaced it carefully. Now she took the Bible and opened it. It was a Spanish Bible, and although the pages were yellow with age, it did not seem that old. Not as old as the lace, maybe even centuries younger. But then a fragment of a piece of paper drifted from it, almost lazily, yet in its idle course it seemed to beg her attention. She picked it up. It was not a piece of the Bible's pages. No, there was handwriting dim with age. Jerry shined the flashlight on it and squinted at the spidery script.

Querida Brianda,
Estoy muy emocionado. Te das cuenta, en tan
solo dos días, ambos haremos la primera
communion. Así, no solamente seremos primos
de sangre, sino que también seremos primos de
espíritu a través de Jesús. ¡Que bien!

She slowly began to translate the Old Spanish. It was hard. Whole sentences remained undecipherable. The word orders were strange. Sometimes she was not sure what the verbs were because they cropped up in funny places. There was something about a veil, a Communion veil Jerry thought, but she wasn't sure. A bit of meaning began to melt out from the paper.

Dear Brianda,
I am so excited. Just think, within two days, on
exactly the same day, we shall both make our
First Communion. So we are not only cousins
by blood but shall be cousins of the spirit
through Jesus. How fine!

How fine indeed! Jerry felt a quickening within her. It was as if a storm of butterflies suddenly rose in a golden flight inside her chest. The paper seemed as fragile as the wings of a butterfly. Time began to slip from its harness. Jerry held the paper and closed her eyes for a second. Instead of blackness or the crazy jig of neon squiggly lines that had danced on the inside of her eyelids, this time she glimpsed a dim light, a light from an unimaginable distance that had traveled like the light of ancient stars.

The House in the Wall
CALLE DE PUERTA VIEJA DE BISAGRA
TOLEDO, SPAIN
JANUARY 1449

❊❊❊

Beatriz

The baby is crying again. I can hardly write this letter to my cousin between his crying and the hinges of the city gates creaking. Well, in truth, I am more accustomed to the city gates than a baby's cry. My room here in our house in the walls is right next to the gates. Those creaks of the hinges have been a part of my life since I was born. It's the baby I am not used to. I just don't see why he had to be born this week of all weeks! The week of my First Communion! I have waited ten years to become a communicant in the church of our Lord and there is the party planned and everything. All those hours I had to spend with Padre Hoya and then Sister Maria Theresa. Sister Maria Theresa has an ugly mole right above her lip with a hair growing out of it. It was very hard to concentrate on the catechism. Sister would ask the questions of, say, the first lesson, and I would answer.

"What must we do to save our souls?"

"To save our souls, we must worship God by faith, hope, and charity. . . ."

And all the time I answer and she bobs her head, that little hair sprouting from the mole waggles about. It is a credit to my powers of concentration that I could learn the catechism so well, and now with this baby yowling? Why, oh, why did little Enrique have to come this week of all weeks? I know this is selfish, but it is really *my* week.

I know that to think this way, so close to the day of my First Communion, is not proper. Sister Maria Theresa is too old to read these sins of my heart. She still thinks that if my feet dare touch the ground when I kneel I shall have to spend thirty minutes in hell having my toes scorched.

The sisters speak of such dark things. There is so

much talk of purgatory. It frightens me. The sisters remind us of how terrible it will be to see the face of God after death if indeed our sins have not been made up for, our "accounts" not reconciled. So sometimes I picture myself waiting in front of God, a faceless God because I cannot imagine his face, but he is holding an account book, a ledger just like the one Papa writes in the payments or debts for his silver orders.

So yes, dearest Brianda, I am bubbling with excitement. Although I think it is so sad that your brother Tomás shall be here in Toledo because of our troubles and not with you in Seville for your Communion. However I shall be sending back with Tomás a special medal that Papa has made for the occasion of your First Communion. My veil is very simple. It has lovely butterflies flying upward as if toward heaven. It is after a design of my great-grandmother Doña Grazia. Yes, she is still alive. She is nearly one hundred years old and she no longer works the bobbins. Another lace maker made it. The veil must look simple. My grandparents insist. For during these times it

is not right for anyone to show their wealth,
especially the family of a tax farmer. And what
with Papa a silversmith, we might invite great
anger.

What is your Communion veil like? How
long is it? Does it come to your shoulders or
below?

"Beatriz! Beatriz! Your cousin Tomás has arrived. You must get ready for dinner."

"Yes, Abuela. Just a minute."

I wish Mama would let me wear my hair up in a crown of braids like the big girls. I love the way they look when they walk around the square on Saturday afternoons. If I shall be old enough to take Communion by tomorrow, why not wear my hair up? Of course, even when I am old enough, Mama and Papa will never let me walk around the square to show me off to possible suitors. We are New Christians and that "parade," as Papa calls it, is considered an Old Christian custom. Funny, isn't it, this New Christian, Old Christian business. How can my great-grandmother Doña Grazia be considered a new anything at nearly one hundred years old!

I hear Mama calling again. "Coming!" I shout,

and rush downstairs. But just as I am passing my grandfather's study, I hear a word that makes me stop: "Granada." I catch my breath. If I press myself into the shadows just outside the study, they will not see me but I can see them. I see Tomás pacing.

"I think, Don Alvaro and Don Diego, that you must consider Granada." That is my cousin Tomás speaking. What is he talking about? Granada? I have to listen. I know it is spying. Yet another sin.

"You, Don Diego, the king recognizes what a fine job you have done collecting for this loan for the country's defenses."

"It is the *pueblo menudo*. . . ." Don Alvaro interrupted. "The little people, it is always the lower classes and Governor Sarmiento who cause the problems for the New Christians."

What does this have to do with Granada? I wonder. What must they consider about Granada?

"Look, hasn't Sarmiento always been hoping for your job, Don Diego, as tax farmer? The resentment has been building against New Christians like ourselves who are successful with good positions, ever since last spring when they passed the pure-blood laws."

I cannot stand this talk of the pure-blood laws. It

sickens me. I have been a Christian my whole life. Mama and Papa have been Christians their whole lives. My grandmother converted and was baptized when she was ten. So why do they call us "New Christians," and impure ones at that? It seems so unfair. Who can help how they were born or who their great-grandparents were? You know, I used to like the word *limpieza*. I liked its sound. I liked the way it felt on my tongue. It felt a bit like what it meant—"clean." But now when they talk about clean pure-blood laws, I hate the word. It is odd how a plain and simple word can be ruined. I must admit the one very good thing about Sister Maria Theresa is that she hates the laws and I think the word, too, now.

I remember soon after the laws had been passed when Sister and I were walking home together from devotions, a town crier was calling out the new rulings. He was announcing how New Christians were no longer permitted to hold public offices because of their lack of pure blood. Sister clapped her hands over my ears and actually shouted at the town crier, "This is foul! This is foul! You have no right to bring this news to the ears of little ones preparing for their First Communion. We are all pure in God's eyes, even sinners like you."

For this alone I know that Sister Maria Theresa will never have to spend one minute in purgatory.

I hear only quiet now.

"Judaizers! They call us Judaizers." What is this word *Judaizer*?

"Judaizer!" Don Diego hisses. "How can they say that? My own grandparents converted long before the massacres of thirteen ninety-one. My own granddaughter is to have her First Communion tomorrow."

"Still they think that we secretly practice the old faith." It is Tomás's voice I hear.

Then my grandfather takes the thoughts right out of my head and gives them words. "And when do they think we do this? When do we 'Judiazers' practice as Jews? One religion takes enough time." He snorts. And I nearly laugh out loud.

Tomás walks to the other end of Grandfather's study, and I cannot hear him so well as the fire in the hearth crackles louder. I strain. It is something about the gates of the city. Then I hear my name as clear as anything. Why would they speak of me?

"Who knows how loyal the sentries at the gates are? That is why it is so good that you live where you do, here in the house in the walls. You can hear the hinges, can't you?"

"Yes, much to Juana's annoyance, and Beatriz too can hear them plainly as her bedroom abuts the east gate's hinges. The walls are thick, but the sound of that iron carries through the stone."

"Well, warn her that she must come to you immediately if she hears the sound of the dead bolts and the ring bolts that they use in the hinges."

I scratch my head. A bad habit just like my grandmother Abuela Maria inherited from her mother. Abuela Maria has to wear a piece of a wig to cover the bare patch. "But why must we listen for the hinge bolts?"

"Because, gentlemen, that means that they are sealing the city to the king, the king and his forces, and that indeed Sarmiento and his rebels will hold Toledo. Then God help the New Christians." Tomás laughs harshly.

Roasted pigeon, not my favorite. I think I'll just eat the olives and the bread if I can get away with it.

"Ah, tomorrow, Beatriz, we shall be eating your Communion cakes. Emilia rises before the sun to bake them, do you not, Emilia?" My mother, Doña

Juana, says, then adds, "Eat the pigeon, dear. You have a big day coming up. And tell us, Tomás, will your family be having Brianda's dinner at your home or that of your grandparents?" And will her veil be utterly beautiful? I wonder.

"Ah, at home. And when I return, I shall give Brianda the lovely St. Francis medal that you send. Yes, that is the saint's name she will choose when she is confirmed in a few years—at least that is what she says now."

"What a perfect name for little Brianda. I remember so well when she came here and she and Beatriz found the wounded bird and, my goodness, she didn't even want Cook to kill the mouse she caught in the pantry," Mama reminisces.

"Oh." Tomás laughs. "I think we have more animals in our home than people. Two hutches of rabbits—none may be slaughtered for eating—countless little canaries in cages, and of course Brianda would like them to fly free."

Everyone is laughing. How can these men be laughing when less than half an hour before they spoke of terrible danger and how I must listen for the creak of the hinges? When are they going to tell me to do that and stop talking about saints' names?

"Beatriz! Tomás has been asking you a question. What is to be your saint's name? Who have you selected?"

"Oh, pardon, Mama. Elizabeth for St. Elizabeth of Hungary," I reply.

"And tell us about her," my mother presses me.

"Yes, Mama. St. Elizabeth was the daughter of a king and she helped the poor and she even built a hospital to tend the sick near her family's castle. And once when she was taking food to some sick poor person, she was stopped and another person looked under her mantle where there was to be food and instead there were roses."

"How's that supposed to help a starving person?" Doña Maria asks.

"Abuela!" I exclaim.

"Just asking. I suppose it was a miracle?" Doña Maria begins to scratch at the top of her head and readjusts a comb. Too late a spot of pink winks through the gray hair.

"Go on, Beatriz, tell what else she is the patron saint of." Mother, would you stop! I want to scream.

"Lace makers just like Doña Grazia," I reply quietly.

"What?" At the very end of the table, next to my grandfather, Don Diego, sits Doña Grazia, my great-grandmother and mother of Doña Maria. Doña Grazia scares me. She rarely speaks, and when she does it is often in a strange language that I do not understand. They say it is a mixture of Spanish and some ancient tongue, and that people in the Juderia of Seville used to speak this. But now she is saying "*What?*" in perfect Spanish.

"Abuela." My grandfather Diego de Luna speaks now. "The saint for whom Beatriz will take her name when she is confirmed is Saint Elizabeth, and she is the patron saint of lace makers. Is that not lovely? Fitting? Doña Maria?" he says, and turns to his wife.

"Miriam! My daughter's name is Miriam!" Abuela Grazia's words are like a cold blade slicing through the air. It is as if a summer day had in the split of a moment turned frigid, as if a blizzard had suddenly blanketed a meadow of wildflowers in snow. We all sit in a stunned silence. Whatever would make my great-grandmother say something like this and with such anger? This little wisp of a thing. She sits at the far end of the table wrapped in layers upon layers of lace. Black lace and gray lace and lavender lace. Her body is so tiny and shriveled, it reminds me of a spider sitting in the middle of its web, a web made of the finest lace. They said that she stopped speaking for a long time after the family left Seville. And now she never wastes words. Sometimes I think it is her very stillness, her silence, that scares me the most.

Once I watched a spider lure a fly into its web. It was early morning in the courtyard and the dew was still on the roses. Sparkling in a corner of the stone wall was a web that appeared as if it had been strung with diamonds. It caught my eye and I was drawn to it, powerlessly drawn to it. And then I saw that I was not the first. Woven into the web was the body of a cricket. All neatly bound up in silk, like a little loaf, waiting to be the spider's next meal. And at that very moment another fly was being drawn into the shimmering latticework. It would have been so easy for me to destroy the web. I might have, too, except Doña Grazia on her two canes had silently come up behind me and whispered, "Beauty! Beauty, a deadly but most lovely beauty. You know I used to take my inspiration from such things as spider's webs and dragonfly wings."

Finally Papa speaks and breaks the silence at the dinner table. "I think it might be time for Doña Grazia to retire." He gets up. "Pablo!" Pablo,

Emilia's son, who helps in the kitchen, comes with Doña Grazia's canes. I watch as she walks with Papa on one side and Pablo on the other. She looks just like a spider now, slowly scuttling out of the room. It is as if she has eight legs: the two God gave her, two canes, and the legs of Papa and Pablo.

Tonight I dream of hinges and spiders. Spiders spinning webs in ancient walls . . . spiders waiting . . . waiting, waiting.

This is all I remember from the day of my Communion. I remember first the sweet smell of my Communion cakes baking. The scent of vanilla swirling up from the kitchen before I was even awake. And then I remember opening my eyes and knowing it was barely morning. It was that time just after dawn when the light slides through the window, thin and gray, and there is always a softness to that light that is soothing to eyes just opened. My dress hung on the clothes tree, stiff and very white. The veil draped on the looking glass was stirred by an invisible wind. I got up and I put the veil on. While still in my night rail I kneeled, clasping my hands with the rosary twined among my fingers, and said my Hail Mary. Sister said I must do this first thing on the morning of my First Communion. I must do this before I spoke a word to anyone. Before I even made water in my chamber pot.

But while I prayed, that sweet smell of the cakes wound its way from the kitchen. It made my mouth water, and I wished that I would not have to wait until the party to eat them. I pictured the cakes in their little suits of sugar frosting and the rose-colored crosses. Emilia, who could not write a word, could inscribe anything in frosting. And then it was time to dress and go to the cathedral. I carried a small bouquet of flowers and a basket with some of my Communion cakes and a small jug of olives. These I would give to the poor as we entered the courtyard of the cathedral through the Puerta de Mollete, the Muffin Gate. For this is where the poor waited to receive food, and on one's First Communion day it was customary to give food to them.

But you see, we never got that far. We never got to the Muffin Gate. I never had my Communion. Just as we stepped round the corner into the Plaza Zocodover, there was a terrible scream. From whose throat it came I am not sure. It could have been Mama's or maybe Grandmother's or maybe even

Papa's. And then I followed their gaze. In the middle of the square hanging feet up was a body. The head covered in blood, long strands like snakes spilling from his stomach. The square was deathly still and there was only one sound being spoken, the name *Juan de la Cibdad*. I knew the sounds, but they did not make sense in my ears. Juan de la Cibdad had come to my little brother's baptism; Juan de la Cibdad had eaten at our table four days ago. What was Juan de la Cibdad doing hanging upside down with red snakes crawling from his belly? Then Papa whispered hoarsely, "Turn around, Beatriz. We are going home. Tomás, take Juana's arm." And Papa took Abuela's arm. And Abuelo, my big grandfather, suddenly seemed to shrink. He put out his hand to touch Papa's elbow as a child might who does not want to lose his mother in a crowded marketplace.

Now that is all that I remember of the day. Papa told us not to leave the house, nor should we open the door for anyone. The rest of the day is like mist to me, until night fell.

Had I heard the hinges? I think not. What would a bolt sound like? But near midnight I was told to dress warmly, and it was not Mama's maid, Matina, who came to help me. It was Mama herself. I put on my heaviest camise and kirtle, and then Mama said, "Another." So I did. And then she fetched my warmest merino dress. And then she said, "Another!"

"Another dress, Mama?" She nodded and said, "Another."

I am wearing three dresses and five shawls. The buttons do not close. I have a satchel with my Bible and that is all. We are leaving Toledo. We shall leave through the wall itself and not through the gates! This astonished me. How do we do that? I ask. There is in our cellar a door that leads into a secret passage that passes directly through the Puerta Vieja de Bisagra that puts us right on the Paseo de Madrid. We are going to Granada. If they have killed the leader of the New Christian community, Juan de la Cibdad, then they can kill us. This is what my father says. And this is very strange—they do not try to whisper behind my back. They do not try to protect me. They do not treat me as a child any longer. I hear everything. I have seen everything. I have seen a dead man, his blood dripping, his guts spilling, hanging upside down in the square of the Zocodover. And now I know I am not a child. Grandfather is speaking to me. "You must go, Beatriz, to your great-grandmother; you must go to Doña Grazia. You must beg her to come with us; you must insist. She refuses to move. No one can budge her."

"But why should I be able to?"

"You must try."

So now I go into her bedroom. She sits straight upright in bed. Her night rail is trimmed in finest lace that has turned creamy with age. From the outside she looks like a confection, frothy and sweet; but her eyes are hard and black, her mouth stitched into a little puckered line. I feel myself being drawn into her web of lace. My feet move on their own, for my mind is numb. I am one of those insects about to be snagged in a silken death. I crawl right up on the bed. "Abuelita!" I whisper. She does not move. Her eyes are sunken. I put out one finger and touch the lace that gurgles up around her neck. She tips over. Abuelita is dead. My little spider grandma collapses against the pillows.

The fire in the grate has gone out, and a sudden draft sucks ashes up the flue. I go to the shuttered windows and open them. A cold wind blows in. The lace on my great-grandmother's gown stirs. She is like the ashes. She will blow away. She will not hang upside down and bloody in the square. I shall never have my First Communion. I do not care. But I do wonder how Brianda looks in her veil.

Chapter 11

❧

"WHAT'S THAT IN your hand?" Constanza had just come into the kitchen from the cook yard. She peered hard at Jerry as if trying to see something through the dimness of a darkening day. But it was morning and the sun was up and Jerry stood barefoot in the kitchen clutching a piece of paper in her hand.

"You tell me." And she held out the letter toward her aunt. Did it sound rude? She didn't care. The words sounded wonderful to Jerry. Slow, but not strangled, not chunks of rock. Constanza took the old piece of paper and looked down at it. She squinted harder, then moved to the desk where she kept orders and picked up a magnifying glass. "Oh," she said suddenly. Jerry noticed a tiny pulse in her temple. Her aunt was muttering something. "'*No me gusta mi mantilla de . . .'* Oh, Lord love a duck, they're always complaining about their veils. Heh!" She snorted and handed the letter back to Jerry. But Jerry was quick. She put her hands behind her back and did not reach for the letter.

"But what is it, Aunt Constanza?" She said the words slowly. The letter began to tremble in her aunt's hands.

"Well, it's just some letter, that's all. Old, old letter. You know, when my sister died—that was years ago—they sent over to me what they couldn't sell. Just old family stuff. Half of it I don't know what it is, what to do with it . . . you know," she added in a tone of dismissal, thrusting the letter out toward Jerry, who now took it.

And that's it, Jerry thought. Just old, old stuff. She looked hard at her aunt, but Constanza did not look back. She was shuffling some papers on her desk. "My, my. I got ten dozen more Communion cakes to bake myself here by tomorrow. Have to get crackin'. I'll let you do the driving tomorrow afternoon when we deliver them—three different churches, one up the valley. Nice windy road. I'll teach you how to downshift on the curves."

❖ ❖ ❖

"You got to keep your eyes on the road, Jerry. I don't think you're concentrating hard enough."

Her aunt was right. She wasn't concentrating hard enough. She was thinking about her aunt, not the road. How her aunt seemed not to know about that letter, not to care. But the problem was that Jerry was beginning to care. Who was Brianda? And who was Beatriz who had written to Brianda? And why, when she had first looked at the letter, couldn't she really translate much of it, and then why did she in some mysterious way now understand the letter? This was not a bad dream, not a good dream, not a dream at all. But what was it and why did her aunt not know anything?

"Watch out!" Constanza roared. A truck was coming their way and Jerry was taking the curve too fast. Somehow they managed to emerge collision free, but they were both breathing hard. "Pull over, child. I'll drive for now. Your mind is someplace else." And that, thought Jerry, was in fact the understatement of the year.

A breeze stirred in the small church and the little girls' veils blew softly around their faces. Jerry could tell that they were debating whether to transfer their bouquets from one hand to another to secure their veils. There were only five first communicants, three little girls and two little boys. The all looked to Jerry to be about second graders. She remembered her First Communion dress. She hated it. And the veil was even worse. Leave it to her mother to come up with something really weird. Her veil was a turban with a scarf attached. She looked more like an Arabian princess than a first communicant in the Roman Catholic Church.

There was to be a party in the refectory afterward, and Constanza had baked the white cakes for it. As she stood now in church, Jerry realized that this fragrance blended perfectly with the baking cakes in the house in the wall, the home of Beatriz in Toledo. After the service Jerry helped her aunt in the refectory serve the cakes and lemonade. The cakes had not just crosses but doves of peace and lilies inscribed in frosting on them. Sinta was there with her family. A cousin of hers had celebrated her First Communion. "You should have come to the movies. It was really good." Jerry smiled and shrugged. "Tomorrow we have a study hall right before sewing. They might let us into the sewing room. So bring your skirt and we could get a head start. Okay?"

Jerry nodded and smiled broadly. Sometimes, she realized, she got sick of smiling. If only a word would come out. Well, they had sort of with Aunt Constanza there in the kitchen when she had demanded—yes, demanded not simply asked—about the letter. "You tell me." She remembered the words. She remembered wondering if they sounded rude. When she had been in the cellar, she never even thought about words and when or if she could speak them. She had a voice when she was in the cellar, and it had been heard. She knew this. When she had opened the trunk, when time flowed back and unimaginable distances suddenly flexed into a brief arc and allowed her to walk into another century and another house, she had a voice. She had spoken. She was not mute. Now if only she could speak so fluently, so freely, upstairs in the light of day.

Perhaps tonight when she was in bed she would try to whisper the questions softly into the night. She had, after all, managed to speak a few sentences to her aunt. Her voice was there. It was somewhere. She just knew it.

Chapter 12

❖❖❖

JERRY LAY IN BED. She had been trying forever to recall the sound of Beatriz's voice,
but for some reason it wasn't working.
And every time she tried to think of a question
to ask, even if she had remembered the girl's
voice, for some reason she thought of her
mother, her mother and the stupid veil she had
concocted for Jerry's First Communion. In her
desperation she had even tried to imagine a
conversation between herself and Beatriz about
Communion veils. It would go something like
this: If you think simple is bad, try silly, try looking like a cross between a desert Arab in a
burnoose and a Hindu swami in a turban for
your First Communion. Take your pick.

But Beatriz and Doña Maria and Doña
Grazia and the rest seemed to recede into some
misty region. Instead there was her mother,

Millie, so fragile, her toothpick arms, her darting glances, with her rapid-fire, breathless speech, always rushing up to you as if she had something desperately important to confide.

Jerry got out of bed now and went to the bureau drawer where she kept a few things in a small cedar box with writing on the lid that said "New Mexico, Land of Enchantment." She opened the box and took out the linen card the nuns had given her at the Catholic Charities home and read again about the friars in Assisi and Padua who were praying, perhaps at this very minute, for her mother.

Outside she heard the rumble of thunder, then a crack of lightning peeled back the dark, and every object was limned in a hot white radiance. On the porch she saw the figure of Constanza. She saw the small bald spot, somehow shocking, like the eye of a hurricane as strands of Constanza's white hair loosed by the wind whipped about her head. A few smudged stars wheeled in the sky and clouds chased after a lopsided moon. Everything was swirling in this night, but Jerry clamped her eyes shut trying to banish the image of those violets eddying around her mother's ankles.

Jerry was still holding the card of the Franciscan

friars in her hand. Assisi! The word jumped out at her. That was the medal Beatriz's father had made for her cousin Brianda as a gift for her Communion. She had seen that medal in the trunk. She was sure. So tarnished it was almost black. She had simply scraped it aside when she had replaced the Bible the first time she had ever opened the trunk.

Jerry waited until she was sure that Constanza had gone to bed. She then took a flashlight. The steady rain outside muffled her footsteps. The temperature had dropped and the air was cold. On the back of a chair was a shawl that she picked up and wrapped herself in. She opened the cellar door and began her descent. The stairs were familiar. She knew that the edge of the third step was cracked. She no longer needed the flashlight. Her eyes were accustomed to the darkness now and she knew the way. It was curious, but not only did the familiar shapes seem to dissolve into the perpetual dusk of the cellar, she also began to feel the slide of time itself.

Outside the stars swirled, and inside once more centuries began to bend. Time curved back as Jerry reached to lift the lid of the trunk. She pushed the

Bible aside. A small, dark disk glowered. She picked it up, licked it, then took the corner of her shawl and rubbed it. The figure of a man emerged. On one shoulder a squirrel was perched, on the other a bird, and the man's head was tilted toward the sky where two more flew. Jerry rubbed a bit harder. The man's mouth was open. It was St. Francis. He was preaching to the birds and all the animals that Brianda had loved. Brianda, who hadn't even wanted the cook to kill a mouse in her pantry. Brianda of Seville . . .

In the House of the Doctor
ON CALLE DE JERONIMO
SEVILLE, SPAIN
APRIL 1480

❖✦❖

Luis

I think it is an awful thing being twelve years old, especially to be twelve years old and the youngest and the only boy. I am left out of everything. I tell my friend Paco this and he says, "So you want to wear dresses and corsets and kirtles like your sisters and weave ribbons in your beautiful hair?" He waves his fingers through his own hair as a girl does. He does not understand. It is not that I want to wear dresses; I just don't like being left out. They all think I am too young, too young to understand anything. But I know a lot more than they think. I know, for instance, that Rosita is secretly seeing Juan Sebastian, a young gentleman of the court. But Juan Sebastian is an Old Christian and we are New Christians, Conversos, and we must marry other Conversos. So Rosita and Juan would be in big trouble if anyone found out. Of course my other sister, Elena, knows. Because girls, especially sisters, cannot keep secrets. Also she knows because Rosita needs Elena's help to make meetings with Juan. I figured this out because I became suspicious when they kept going to the convent to help embroider the robe of the Macarena Virgin, which will be carried through the streets during the Holy Week procession to the cathedral. But Rosita does not work as long on the robe as she says nor as often. I cannot believe that my mother and father don't suspect anything. But they don't. This is why children can get away with a lot—because their parents are so unsuspecting.

But I am cleverer than my sisters. I don't say stupid things like I am going to church to light a candle for Abuela Yolanda, who died last year. No. When Papa sends me on an errand to, say, the herbalist on the Calle de Hierba, I add on a few errands of my own. Papa is a doctor and he sends me often because he likes only the freshest herbs and compounds. Lately Papa has been sending me on lots of errands—errands that keep me away from our house for maybe two hours or more. Just yesterday I had to first go to the herbalist for some theriac. Then I had to go to the olive dealer several streets away for some unripened olives. Papa uses the oil of such olives to dissolve myrtle berries. This is a cure for worms. And every child in Seville, I think, has worms these days. You see them scratching their behinds. My sisters and I have never ever had worms because Papa treats us with what is called a vermifuge three times a year, made from the myrtle oil and some powders. We have to drink it and it makes us spend hours in the privy. I think having worms might be better.

Today I have to go on one of my least favorite errands—to the Convent of Santa Ines on Calle Doña Maria Coronel. I do not like this convent. Some of the nuns are really crazy there. And that is why I have to go: to deliver the fresh pursalane and the aloe vera and then tell them about the egg whites for the blistering, although they should know all this by now. You see, these are the nuns who devote themselves to the memory of a noble woman, Doña Maria Coronel. They celebrate her chastity, for she deliberately disfigured her face with burning oil when King Pedro I demanded her as his mistress. To this day many of the nuns do the same. Their wounds become infected. The disfigurement is not required to join the order, but the new mother superior is said to encourage it. This woman, Mother Angelica, is a cousin of Friar Torquemado, the confessor to Queen Isabella. I once heard Papa say that Friar Torquemado was not quite right in his mind. So I guess it must run in the family, because since Mother Angelica came to this convent there are many more disfigurements. Papa has gently tried to speak to her about this, about how these young women could better serve Jesus if they were healthy. But she says it is a test of their faith. She is so proud in her disfigurement. Is not this kind of pride also a sin?

"Luis, dear boy."

"I have the pursalane and the aloe vera." I put

the package into Mother Angelica's hands as quickly as I can. I try to look only at her hands.

"Bless you, child. Bless you."

There is one very strange thing about the older nuns who disfigure themselves. Their skin never wrinkles in the normal way but is unnaturally shiny on the surface. But beneath I sense a withering. I do not know what else to call it. Mother Angelica's face is so weird. I can see even hidden in the shadows of her wimple, that single eye peering out, the right eye, for the left is gone. The empty socket puckers into a pit of red crimpings like a seam in which the threads had been drawn too tight. Her face is all pulled to one side. Half of the upper lip is gone, melted away like tallow.

"Papa says if this does not work, he will send over a lotion of wine and myrrh."

"Oh yes. How kind. Yes, my dear, yes."

How can her voice sound so normal coming out from such a monstrous face? I turn and run down the street. And you know what? This is the strangest. I feel her eye following me—not the one that is there, not the right one. But the left one that was boiled out.

When I get home, I head for the cellar room where Papa grinds the herbs into powders. "Where are you going?" Mama shrieks. "Why are you back so soon?" Mother asks, and touches the St. Francis medal at her throat. "You can't go down there yet," she barks. "Go outside and play."

I feel my face harden. I hate this. More and more they treat me like a baby; more and more I am having these feelings of being left out. Then I hear footsteps coming up from the cellar. It's Papa who comes through the door first, Don Gabriel follows him, then José Catalan and Gaspar and Isaac Alonso. What is this? What is going on in the cellar? None of these men is a doctor, or an apothecary.

But when the last man comes, I nearly gasp out. It is my uncle Tomás Mendez, the repostero major, the king's chief butler. What is my uncle doing here?

Mama starts to speak. "I am sorry—"

Papa breaks in. "I think the time has come, Brianda."

"Yes," says Uncle Tomás, and then in a lower voice, "he turns thirteen next month, does he not? He would be bar mitzvahed had he studied."

Bar what? Studied what? I don't know what they are talking about.

"All right, gentlemen." Papa is brisk. "I think you should take your leave in the usual manner. Don Gabriel, you first from the front door. Remember the packet of theriac powders I gave you. Hold it prominently." Don Gabriel is already on his way out. "José, from the back door, and Gaspar, you through the courtyard. Your brother Isaac from the front door in five minutes. Tomás, you will wait and take a glass of wine. I have a good new bottle of *tinto*. We shall explain together to Luis. Come, Brianda; come, Luis; come, Tomás." I follow Papa to the cellar.

Everything looks just the same. Papa's worktable where he keeps his mortars and pestles for the grinding is in place. The little coal brazier for boiling herbs still glows. On a shelf in jars filled with spirits, organs of various animals float, waiting for Papa's dissection tools. Papa walks over to a cupboard where he keeps splints. He takes out a long, rectangular box.

"Come here, my son."

I watch and am completely mystified as Papa takes from the box a small skullcap and puts it on.

Tomas also puts one on and then, to my surprise, they place one on my head. Then Papa begins speaking words in a language I have never heard.

"Baruch ata Adonai Elohainu melech ha'olam malbish arumim."

"Papa, what are you saying?"

"Blessed are You, Lord our God, Ruler of the universe, who clothes the naked." Don Miguel pauses. "That is the language of our faith, Luis. I am just learning it. It is Hebrew, and I just said the blessing for wearing a new piece of clothing." He taps the skullcap he has just placed on my head. "You see, I know so few blessings and words in Hebrew." I look surprised. "You think because I am a doctor I know everything? Oh no, I am just starting to learn. Tomás as well, and look, he is the secretary to the king."

"What do you learn, Papa?"

"We learn how to be Jews."

"Jews? We are to be Jews?" I am completely confused.

"We were Jews once long ago—your great-great-grandparents—but we were forced to convert, and now as Conversos, as New Christians, they begin to treat us worse than when we were Jews. So many of us think, what kind of religion is this where they now make laws against the New Christians, where they persecute us, often violently, and try to exclude us?"

My own father feels excluded. This very thought sparks like tinder in my head. I thought only kids felt excluded.

"How do you mean, Papa? Who is being left out?"

"Don Gabriel, an alderman. Fray Alonso Hoyeda says Conservos cannot hold office."

"I know about him, Papa, but everyone says that friar is crazy."

"He *is* crazy. And he has great influence with Friar Torquemado."

"Queen Isabella's confessor."

"Yes. There were troubles three years ago. You might have been too young to remember. The *menudos* resented that the Conversos had many of the high-paying jobs in court. Pressure was brought to bear on the king, and the king agreed to write to the pope in Rome asking for permission to establish a council of inquisition."

"What's that?"

"The Inquisition is to be a group of men from the

church who would look into matters of faith to be sure that everyone practices the true faith, the faith of the Roman Catholic Church, because some Conversos were suspected of secretly practicing their old religion."

"But Papa, you are practicing your old faith."

Don Miguel nodded somberly. "But do I want to belong to a faith that preaches hatred?" He smiles reassuringly. "Don't worry. We shall be careful."

I touch the medal of St. Francis of Assisi just like the one Mama wears. She had given it to me on the occasion of my First Communion. "That is why," Papa says, "you must continue to wear your medal. We must give appearances of our Christianity." Papa pauses and looks troubled for a moment. "Besides, the medal was a gift of love and love does not change. St. Francis loved all things, and there is always more to learn from loving than hating." He brushes his thumb lightly down my cheek. "But do not fret, Luis. So far the king has not appointed the men to the council of the Inquisition. It is Tomás's feeling that the king wants none of this. But in the meantime, we men like Tomás and Don Gabriel and Don Gaspar and Isaac and Don José Catalan have indeed come back to the faith of our fathers.

We want to be Jews even if we must be secret ones. And so we plan a Seder."

"Secret Jews," I whisper. "Do Rosita and Elena know this secret?" Papa nods. So at last I am included in something. But it feels scary.

❖

My part is coming up. In another minute Papa will ask me to say the four questions—that is my job as the youngest at the Seder table. But the problem is, no one can remember what the fourth question is. No one at this table has ever been to a Passover dinner before. I see these grown men with gray in their hair fumbling for words. It is not just the four questions that they are unsure about. There are many other things as well. But the men try to piece together what they have heard and what they think they might have heard. But still the dinner is nice.

"Ready, Luis?" Uncle Tomás asks.

"Yes, *Tío*." I clear my throat and begin. "Why is this night different from all the other nights? Because on all other nights we eat leavened bread and on this night we eat only unleavened bread, matzo." And I hold up a piece of the unleavened bread that Mama baked two days before, at night when the maid was gone and would not notice. Next question. I take a big breath and hold up a horseradish root: "Why on this night are we supposed to eat especially bitter herbs?"

And now the third question. I pick up a piece of parsley and hold it by the stem: "Why on this night do we eat parsley?"

José Catalan breaks in. "I think the proper question—although, Luis, you are doing excellently—is 'Why on this night do we dip twice the parsley in the salt water?'" I nod and begin the question again.

But still no one can remember the fourth question. Tomás said that the questions would be answered as the story of the Jews' flight from Egypt was retold, and this is the part of the Seder, the story of the Exodus, that most interests me. Their flight from slavery. But it gives me a shudder to think about those men Papa spoke of, the men of the Inquisition. They might be able to have the power to make slaves out of the very people who sit at this table, make them slaves or perhaps kill them. And then we too, like those in ancient Egypt, would have to flee.

As I eat the food, I begin to see that this is the strangest meal that I have ever eaten. It is not just that the food is different but that each dish is a symbol for something else. The parsley dipped in salt water is supposed to remind people of the sweat and tears of the enslaved Jews of Egypt. The green parsley itself is a symbol of hope and the coming of spring. There are certain times when we are to drink wine from our cups, but no one is quite sure when. But, still, I think, even though we are in the cellar, I have never seen such a beautiful table. Mama laid the table with the best linens, and over this is a cloth of the most beautiful lace that had been made by a cousin's great-grandmother. So it doesn't really matter to me if the men cannot remember everything about this meal called Seder, because now I no longer feel left out. Now I feel that I belong to something older than time and bigger than Spain, more important than kings and queens and more precious than all the riches and relics of any cathedral.

This is my favorite part of the meal: At the end we all stand up and, raising our wine cups, say together the words "Next year in Jerusalem!" In that moment I really do feel something in me, some unnamable part, maybe my soul, join with those ancient ones of the Bible with the little children, their mothers, their fathers, the grandparents who stood on the edge of the Red Sea and waited for it to part. *Jerusalem*—what a lovely sounding word. It is like bells in my ears. I think that when I grow up, if I ever marry and have a daughter, I shall name her Jerusalem. It would be the most beautiful name in the world.

But I think Rosita will be the first of us married. I see her sneaking out to meet Juan Sebastian. I can't believe Mama! Can she not tell that Rosita is going out to meet a boy? Under her scarf my sister has her hair piled high and I think she has rouged her cheeks. You don't go to the convent like that. I plan to follow her.

As soon as Rosita rounds the corner after leaving the Convent of the Incarnation and steps into an alley, she takes off her scarf. I see it all from a niche in the wall of the alley that is a perfect fit for a small boy like me. I see her pull out a shiny piece of obsidian from the pocket of her kirtle and peer into the blackness. She is pleased with her reflection. I could almost hear her heart skip a beat, however, for when she looks up she sees two nuns walking toward her. They look up and smile at her, terrible, ghoulish, lipless smiles. They are from the convent of Santa Ines. "Bless you, child," they whisper, almost conspiratorially.

Rosita begins to thread her way through narrow streets to another alley. I shadow her expertly. She turns down an alley with no name, but in the middle of a dark stone wall there is a rust-colored door. She enters it and I am left outside. A terrible feeling creeps through me. An icy fear. I am so frightened for Rosita suddenly. I turn and run.

❖

Last year when I walked like this behind my parents and between my two sisters to midnight mass on Christmas Eve, I was shorter than both Rosita and Elena. Now I am taller, nearly as tall as Papa. And last year when I walked to Mass I had been a Christian, and this year I am a Jew. But I shall take Communion as I always do. I shall kneel in prayer alongside Mama and Papa and my sisters. My prayer, however, will be much different. The words on my lips will be those of the Paternoster and the ones in my heart will be the Hebrew ones I have learned in the past few months, those of the Shema. Tonight after the mass, after we return to our house on the Calle de Jeronimo, Papa leaves by the back door through the courtyard. He will wind his way through the dimmest alleys to the church of San Salvador, the church where José de Catalan and Don Gabriel still serve on the governing body. Pedro Fernandez Benedeva, a deacon of the church and father of one of the church priests, will meet with them. He will give a report on the weapons he has brought into the cellar of his house. The men are preparing. I have followed Papa maybe thirty times since September, when it was found out that indeed men had been appointed to the tribunal of the Inquisition. Now on this Christmas Day the men of the tribunal have finally arrived in Seville. But Papa and his conspirators will be prepared. Arms have already been distributed to many important Conversos. All I know is that the inquisitors must not be allowed to take office. For this will be worse than when the pharaohs ruled in Egypt.

I hide in a tree in the neighboring courtyard where I can watch and know when the men have all entered the church, and then I sneak into the reliquary of the church to listen. The shadows are thick and I do not like to think what is inside the boxes and small caskets that rest in the niches. They are holy relics. In one there is a finger of St. Sebastian, and in another a piece of hair from St. Jude. Death swims around me, but this is the only place where I can hear what Papa and his conspirators say. They are in the cellar beneath me and I can listen through a grate in the floor. I have listened over the weeks and heard the men speak of Jews and New Christians who have been tortured and killed in other cities. So I know that I have nothing to fear from the bones and organs of dead saints. No, it is just the living that I fear. But tonight the men take a long time to get inside the church and it is cold up in the tree. At last they are inside and I get ready to jump from my perch, but just then shadows slice across the doors of the church. I am petrified. I cannot take a breath.

"This way!" a voice hisses.

"Juan Sebastian," another calls in a low whisper.

Juan Sebastian! What is Juan Sebastian doing here? He knows! Fool that I am. I had thought for a long while that Rosita had stopped seeing him, but a month ago I suspected they were seeing each other again. What has she told him now?

I am paralyzed in a waking nightmare. Time is slow, moments seem endless. I see men, the king's men, go into the church. I hear shouts, but they sound muffled and now Papa . . . Papa is first. His hands are bound. His face an eerie white. A ribbon of blood curls down my papa's cheek. The other men follow. I begin to scream, but no sound comes out.

I know that I have to get back to our house and warn Mama. And just as I turn the corner, my heels grind into the cobbles. I am too late. One moment stretches into endless ones as I watch Mama and Rosita and Elena led away. Elena and Rosita are put into a separate wagon, and I hear the police chief direct the driver to take them to the Convent of the Sacred Virgin, many leagues out of the city of Seville. Mama, however, is to be taken to the office of the Inquisition. So I follow. I do not know where such an office is, but I certainly have not imagined that the wagon would stop at a wine shop behind the Plaza Major. There are three wagons lined up outside the shop—all with prisoners, their hands bound and now cloth sacks covering their heads. And there is something very curious I notice. The wheels of the wagons have been wrapped in cloth as well as the feet of the horses. The horses' mouths have been muzzled. The door to the wine shop opens and the prisoners are led in.

That is the last time I see my parents until nearly two months later, on February 6, 1481.

But I have learned my first lesson of the Inquisition: The Inquisition comes in silence.

It did not take long for them to rename our street. It was soon called La Calle de Muerte, the street of death. It was named after Mama and Papa, burned at the stake in the first auto-da-fé of the Inquisition. Within days of their arrest, everyone knew that it was because of Rosita that the conspirators were discovered. But I still do not believe Rosita was truly a traitor. She loved Juan Sebastian. She trusted him. But what does it matter now? I live between the shadows, in a time between time. I sleep in the old house of the lepers. No one comes near there. It is the safest place I can be, really. If I were discovered, they would throw me into prison. Girls they send to convents, but boys of my age— and I am soon to be fourteen—they send to prison. And where are these prisons? No one knows for sure, but it is said there are caves and dungeons beneath the city.

I have lost count of the number of autos since

that first one in which my mother and father burned. It is now April. Holy Week, and I have heard that more than two hundred Conversos have been put to the stake. The king and queen no longer attend every single one as they did in the beginning. Even death has become slightly boring to them. Of course, when someone very important is to be "relaxed," they attend. Yes, that is what the sentence of burning at the stake is officially called, "relaxed," because no member of the church must be directly linked to the shedding of blood. So the heretic is "relaxed," or handed over by the tribunal of the Holy Office of the Inquisition to the police, who carry out the sentence. And at each auto-da-fé the priest reads from the text of the Gospel of St. John: "If a man abide not in me, he is cast forth as a branch and is withered: and men gather them and cast them into the fire, and they are burned."

It all works out very properly. It is not only a religion of great mystery and sacred relics but one of great convenience and practicality. Lying is essential now. Lying is the faith. Lying helped murder my parents. I shall never forget that first auto-da-fé, the one on the sixth day of February.

All week I had watched from the shadows as the

chief of police directed the workers in raising the wooden stakes by the *quemadero*, the place of burning. I saw Paco there with his father the day that they raised the statues of the four prophets at each corner of the *quemadero*. I heard someone say that indeed Paco's father had contributed the money for the statues. I remembered thinking, Why would they want the prophets to decorate such a place? But then I thought, as I do a thousand times a day now, Nothing makes sense any longer.

On the morning of February sixth one would have thought it was a festival day. Food vendors were out, and jugglers and acrobats. And soon the procession began. A priest mounted a platform and, as he raised his arms, everyone fell to their knees and began reciting the Paternoster. I did as well, but the words became jumbled in my head. Hebrew, Latin, Spanish collided together on my tongue. How could I believe that there was a God to pray to? How could I believe that there was a thing called faith? How could anything have meaning if the word *faith* had become part of an act to kill? Auto-da-fé—act of faith. Act in which people are burned to death. When I looked up from the prayer, I saw two carts drawn by donkeys. In each cart there were three people. At first I was relieved. I did not see Mama or Papa. But then a coldness began to creep over me as I realized what I was actually seeing. It felt as if my blood was congealing in my veins. My heart did not race, no, quite the opposite. I think it perhaps slowed and might have even stopped for a second as I realized that indeed I was looking directly at my parents. They were passing not thirty feet from me, but they had been transformed into something almost unrecognizable. They looked if not dead, unreal, like figures of effigies. Their eyes were sunken and fixed in their sockets, registering nothing. And on their gaunt bodies hung these oddly comical clothes. They wore tall, pointed hats and the tunics called *sanbenitos*. Embroidered on the tunics by the good nuns of the convent where my sisters had often helped were figures of devils and hideous monsters leaping from the flames.

"That's to remind them," said a bent old lady by my elbow, pointing at the gruesome embroidery.

"To remind them of what?" I asked.

"To remind them, child, of where their poor souls will go if they do not confess and repent."

Hope suddenly swelled inside me. "You mean

they can confess and repent and be saved?"

"Well, of course, my dear. You watch."

So I watched as my mother and father and the four other prisoners mounted the platform and were led to the stakes, where kindling had been piled. An immense white cross stood in the middle, and at this early hour of the morning the shadows cast by it were still long.

"When do they ask them to repent and confess?" I asked.

"Oh, soon, I should think." The old lady turned to a companion. "When do you think, Maria?"

"Oh, look, there goes Friar Torquemado now. Up the steps. He will ask them. The queen's confessor himself. My! My!" She sighed in wonder.

Now I prayed. "Please, God, if there is a god, make my parents confess, make them say anything. Please, God." But when I looked up again, I saw that my mother's head seemed to hang oddly to one side, like a wilted flower collapsed on its thin stalk. "What happened?" I asked.

"What do you mean, what happened?" the old lady asked.

"The lady at the stake, she looks as if she has fainted."

"No, no, she's confessed. They have shown her mercy."

"But she looks"—I struggled to form the words—"she looks dead." The two old women lifted their hands to their mouths and giggled as if they were shy, slightly flirtatious young señoritas.

"But she *is* dead," the one named Maria finally said.

"She is dead? But I don't understand. I thought you said they were showing her mercy."

"They did. They garroted her, broke her neck. It is ever so much less painful than burning, child. It is very merciful."

"But . . ."

At that moment I heard a crackling. "Oh, look, Maria, they've lit the fires. Oh, they must have poured grease on the kindling."

"On the sinners, my dear, as well. Look at them."

Within five seconds the flames leaped twenty feet in the air, and the roar of the inferno drowned out the cheers of the crowd. Ashes began to swirl up on drafts of air, and columns of smoke like knobby fingers poked at a blue and perfect sky.

That was the day my parents burned.

❖ ❖ ❖

It is Holy Week in Seville. Always during this week there is a special feeling that seems to seep through the city, through the neighborhoods, and even into the narrowest alleys. There is anticipation. This sense of the possibility of transformation. There is a belief that through these days of the Passion of Christ, something deep within each person will change. And so indeed the city changes quietly, subtly, as if awaiting this new spirit. In the workshops of artisans, new images of the Virgin, the Virgin of Macarena, are carved. The artisans pay special attention to the Virgin's tears. The tears are the hardest part of the sculpting and they are often painted in silver or gold leaf so they will sparkle. For the Virgin is only represented in her sorrow, crying at the death of her son. It is through her tears and his wounds that transformation is expected. I wait now near the cathedral, for it is Maundy Thursday. This is the most important day. It is the day of humbleness, when kings and rich men are supposed to wash the feet of beggars, and so the beggars line up in front of the massive doors of the cathedral. Their feet are horny with calluses and some festering with pus, toes gnarled from a lifetime without shoes. I line up too. It is risky. I could be discovered, but I wear an urchin's cap down over my eyes. I see Don Olivares, Paco's father, the same man who paid for the statues of the prophets of the *quemadero* where my parents burned; he is the head of one of the brotherhoods that carries the floats in the procession. He carries a cross. But he will set it down at the entrance of the cathedral and will take a bowl of water to wash the beggars' feet. And with this act of humility he shall assure himself a place in heaven. But he does not listen to the gentle gasps of the beggars as their poor feet are washed. No. He listens for the voices of the common folk who say, "Ah, there goes Don Olivares; he is one of the richest men in the province and look at him now on his knees." Yes, I want to look at him on his knees and say, "You will still burn in hell."

I did not wait for the Brotherhood of the Silence and Great Mystery, which was the one of Don Olivares. For just before they came, another group arrived, a handful of women in black scarves carrying candles. They were in fact from the Convent of Santa Ines, and even the statue of the Virgin that they carried had been disfigured. But the wounds carved into her cheeks had been studded with paste jewels. Such is supposedly the transformation of those who suffer. What stupidity!

The sound of the *saeta*, the strange musical prayer that seemed like a moan rather than a song, rose in the air as the women passed. I recognized the wife of the herbalist where I often went to fetch theriac for Papa, but then just behind her were some nuns. One nun was leading another by the hand, for she was blind. And then I felt a gasp tear from the deepest part of me. A shriek froze on my breath. And I thought I had seen the worst. I had not. For there a few feet from me, her face dripping flesh like melted candle wax, her eyes gone, the empty sockets crinkled as peach pits—there was Rosita, my sister.

My city used to smell of orange blossoms, but it now has a strange odor. It is the smell of burning flesh. For indeed they did not even stop the autos during Holy Week, and when I saw my sister I smelled scalded skin and seared eyeballs.

It is only a matter of time until I am discovered. But tonight I have decided I shall leave. The smell, the smell I must get away from, the foul stench. There is only one town that is safe anymore. That is

Granada, still held by the Moors, and I think I remember that Papa said that our relatives from Toledo went to the Moorish city many years ago. I shall try to find them. Yes, it is risky and dangerous, but honestly I now fear nothing. Once you have smelled the flesh of your own parents burning, what else could there be to fear? Nothing. Absolutely nothing. It is time for me to step out of the shadows.

Chapter 13

❖❖❖

JERRY BLINKED AS she walked upstairs. Outside the world had turned a dazzling white. The fence posts of the cook yard wore snowy white caps. The branches of the apricot trees hung heavy with their mantles of snow. Constanza, bundled in a sheepskin coat, her head tied in a scarf under her Navajo black hat, was raking out an oven. Jerry peered at her through the window as she threw a pinch of bread into the hornos. A draft caught a puff of ash and sucked it out of the oven. A thin streak of smoke uncurled like a finger. Jerry felt a bone-pricking shiver rack through her. She did not smell bread. *That was the day my parents . . .* "No!" And she said the word loudly and very clearly as she stood in the kitchen.

"Whatcha saying no about?" Constanza was in the kitchen now, stomping her feet on the mat. She untied her scarf and took off her hat, the brim of which had collected its own little snow-drifts.

"No." Jerry felt her eyes grow wide and round in astonishment. "I am not going to church anymore."

"Fine, dear, suit yourself," Constanza said softly.

Is this going to be like the letter? Jerry thought. Was she going to be left standing in the kitchen in a puddle of the melted snow her aunt brought in, saying, "That's it"? She wasn't saying simply no to church. "Aunt Constanza," Jerry said, "listen to me."

Constanza turned slowly around. A new alertness in her eyes. She licked her lips and then very deliberately pulled out a chair from the kitchen table. She sat down and took a deep breath, then folded her hands on top of the table. Despite the calm, folded hands and the steady gaze, Jerry could see that Constanza was nervous. "Yes, Jerry," she said quietly. "Do you have something you want to tell me?"

And so Jerry began to tell.

Hours passed. She had missed most of her morning classes. It had begun to snow again, so it seemed pointless to go. The sun that had been so bright was swallowed up into a sky swirling with snow. "It's a blizzard out there," Constanza said when Jerry came back up from the cellar. She was carrying something in her hand. Constanza leaned forward while scratching her head. "So what you got there?" She spoke in a low whisper.

Jerry set down the letter, then the piece of stained lace. She unfolded the lace and took out the medal with the man and the squirrel perched on his shoulder. There was also a piece of shell she had found with a hole in it. It looked as if it had once been strung to wear as a pendant.

Constanza's long fingers reached out, her hand shaking. She touched the medal. "St. Francis," she said softly, then looked up at Jerry. "So you learned all this—all that you were telling me—from these things—this lace, this letter, this medal of St. Francis?"

"In a way. It was the beginning." Jerry knew it would be hard to explain what had happened in her mind. Constanza looked down at the objects on the table and touched one, then the other, sometimes picking up one to look at it more closely. Jerry waited. She had nothing more to say. She hoped Constanza would not ask for anything more, any reasons or explanations of how she had come to know what she knew. It was not a dream. She thought that Constanza understood this. Minutes passed. No one spoke. Then finally Constanza rubbed the patch on her head. "Well, yes, a beginning. It's a beginning," she said, and got up to leave for church.

She put on her sheepskin coat. Slapped the hat on her head once more and anchored it with a scarf. Just before she walked out the door, she paused and looked back at Jerry, who was still sitting at the table. Jerry saw a guttering light in her aunt's eyes, almost a flicker of fear, or was it embarrassment? Her strong, straight-backed aunt suddenly seemed slightly hunched and smaller. Jerry saw her bite softly on her bottom lip as if she were about to say something, but somehow her words were lost.

"It's all right, Aunt Constanza, you go on to church. It's okay."

Jerry looked down at the things she had brought up from the cellar. The piece of shell looked out of place. It didn't look as if it belonged. But it was lovely. Jerry got up to get a piece of string. She cut a length off the ball that Constanza kept in the cupboard, threaded the shell onto it, and tied it around her neck. She liked the feel of it at the base of her throat. In another minute she heard the door slam, and when she looked out the window, she saw that the twilight was now slipping into a darkness studded with snowflakes. She watched her aunt as the old lady bent herself against the wind and punched through the blizzard to her truck.

Chapter 14

❊

I T SNOWED ALL NIGHT, and when she got up the next morning and looked out her window, she saw that the hornos had vanished entirely under huge drifts of snow. There were a few telltale feathers of smoke hovering over the drifts, and that was the only sign that beneath bread was still baking. She saw Constanza with a shovel and quickly hopped out of bed. How was that old lady going to move all that snow?

In less than five minutes she was dressed and getting her coat off the hook.

"You need a hat, foolish girl!" Constanza looked up at her niece. "Go in and get a hat if you want to help. No school today, huh? Snow day. Lucky you. You can help me all day if you like. I have a lot of orders to deliver. Time you learned how to drive in snow."

Jerry looked hard at her aunt. Drive in snow! Was she crazy? If there was no school because of snow, why in the name of God did her aunt think this was a good day for a driving lesson? "Go in and get your hat," Constanza cawed. "What good will you do me if your hair gets wet and you get sick?" Jerry turned to go back in.

They worked together in the cook yard all morning. It did not take them long to excavate the hornos. For the first time her aunt allowed Jerry to build the new fires for the second batches, putting in the fruitwood one piece at a time, as her aunt instructed. When the wood had burned down completely, the ashes were raked out with the wet cloth and the pans of bread slid onto the oven's floor. Hot rocks were placed inside with damp cloths over them to block any cracks in the stove, and another rock was placed on top of the smoke hole. By midmorning the supply of split wood had run out. "Come on," Constanza said. "You might as well learn how to split wood."

Jerry walked with her aunt over to the woodpile, which first had to be broomed off to even reveal a log. Then her aunt put a short log on end atop the chopping block and took her splitting maul.

"Watch me. You try to swing this maul in a big circle so it comes down hard." Jerry watched her aunt begin the swing. Her head and eyes stayed focused on the wood. There was a *thunk*, then a *thwack* sound, and the log popped apart into equal pieces.

"Now you try it." Constanza stepped aside. "Keep the swing at full arm's length, then you won't chop off any of yourself."

Lovely, thought Jerry. There was another *thunk* and a *thwack*.

"You're a natural." Constanza gave a little cackle. "Too bad for you. You can split the rest of that pile. I'm taking a rest before I put in the second batch."

Within minutes Jerry was sweating. She removed her coat and hung it on a fence post. It took her the better part of an hour to split the pile. She took the split pieces in the wheelbarrow, which was not easy to negotiate through the snow, to the ovens where they had built the new fires. She saw her aunt coming out of the house again with the dough for the second batch. She set down the plank with the flattened loaves and reached into her pocket for one of the little dough balls. Jerry was still breathing hard from her labors, and when the word came out it sounded almost more like a breath or small gasp than an actual word. But Constanza heard it: "Why?"

"Well, now, that's a good question." She looked down at the little dough ball in her hand, chuckled softly, then shrugged. "Not sure, really. I just do it. Superstition, I suppose. My mother did it. Her mother did it and her mother's mother did it. Indian stuff, maybe. Some of my folks came from the Yucatán. I guess that means some of yours did too, seeing as you're my great-grand-niece."

Chapter 15

❖❖❖

"NOW THE LAST THING you ever want to do if you start to skid on a patch of ice is put on the brakes. No. What you do is steer right in the direction you are skidding and let up on the gas."

Jerry nodded and concentrated on the road. The roads didn't seem too bad except they were climbing higher and higher on this mesa road and the banks of snow were getting deeper. They had already delivered orders to the country club as well as three restaurants downtown. But Constanza had some special customers.

"We're going to see Margaret Santangel. She's sort of a relative." Jerry started to look at her aunt. "Keep your eyes on the road. You're not that good yet. And shift. The grade gets steep here." Jerry pushed in the clutch, shifted, and then eased up on the clutch. She was getting better. "Margaret—let me see. She's a relative on your great-grandfather's side, I think. There were some cousins—Navajo ones that married into some Pueblos. I can't remember. Anyhow they're having some corn dance or something up here. Lot of tourists come. So I'm bringing them up some bread to freeze. Tourists don't know whether it's been frozen or not. Give the fresh stuff to Margaret. She's a nice gal."

Gal! Jerry wondered. If Margaret Santangel was a gal, Jerry thought, she herself must be an embryo. Margaret was the absolutely oldest person that Jerry had ever seen. She was almost as dark as a prune and about as wrinkled. Her legs appeared to bow into a near O in her loose-fitting pants, and she wore a sweatshirt that said "Go Tigers." Her house in the pueblo on top of the mesa was small and neat as a pin.

"Do you like Twinkies, dear?" the old woman asked. Jerry wasn't sure what she meant, but she nodded, and Margaret went into her kitchen and brought out a cellophane package. Indeed inside was one of the small buns filled with cream.

"How can you eat that crap, Margaret, when I bring you good pueblo bread?" Constanza demanded.

"My teeth, they been hurting."

"What teeth?"

Margaret giggled. "Well, it's the gums in between the two I have." She grinned and turned toward Jerry. Margaret's gums were the exact color of blue corn.

"So you're not going to eat my bread?"

"No, of course I will. I dunk it and it's just fine. But youngsters like Twinkies. I keep them on hand for my grandchildren."

There was a knock on the door. Margaret said something in a language that Jerry didn't understand. The door swung open and another lady nearly as old as Margaret entered. Margaret began speaking in the strange language. Constanza seemed to know the lady and joined in. Then Constanza turned to Jerry. "They're speaking Tewa—Old Tewa." She then turned back to the woman who just arrived. "Grace, this is my niece Jerry." Grace smiled and bobbed her head and then resumed talking in Tewa. Margaret brought out some more Twinkies and some of the bread that Constanza had brought and put on a tea kettle.

The women continued to babble away in Tewa. Jerry couldn't help but wonder how, if Margaret was such a distant relative, Constanza had learned to speak this language. Margaret got up to get a picture of one of her grandchildren. The framed photograph rested on the mantle between a crucifix and two funny little figurines no more than four or five inches tall caught in some antic dance. "Ah, you like my koshare doll?" Margaret didn't wait for Jerry to ask what a koshare doll was. "Everyone makes big fusses about kachina dolls. Me, I like the koshares—the mischief dolls, Delight Makers, some call them. They do everything we might want to do but are scared to try. See this one. The two are dancing and he's trying to peek under her skirts and she's about to kick him." All the old ladies laughed heartily. "I got a golfer one too in the back room. He's a cute fellow. But I don't play golf. I might give it to a nephew who's got the golf bug." Margaret sighed. "I like the koshare dances at the corn festival. Those are the best. You know they do everything that is rude. Not real nasty. Not devil nasty—not white-guy religion—just rude and funny—old Pueblo religion. Here, let me get this one down for you so you can have a look." As she walked by the table, she brushed against the plate with the Twinkies and bread on it and it fell to the floor and shattered. "Oh, my my my! So clumsy." She went to get a broom and dustpan. Before she could really think, Jerry jumped up.

"I'll do that." The words slipped out easily. She took the broom and began sweeping the pieces into a pile near the door. She bent down and swept the pile into the dustpan, but then there were a few little bits and pieces of dust. Jerry put her hand on the door and began to open it to sweep out the rest.

"Oh no!" Constanza said, and then stopped herself suddenly. She began scratching the thin patch on her head.

"What's the matter?" Margaret asked.

Jerry looked at her aunt. "Oh, just an old superstition. Never brush dirt across the threshold," Constanza replied.

"Oh, for heaven's sakes!" Grace batted the air with her hand. "I had an old aunt, over in Tucumcari. She did the same thing. Used to scold me all the time. Never sweep dirt out the door!"

"Margaret," Constanza said suddenly. "Jerry's been asking me 'bout old times."

"What old times?" Margaret said, fiddling with the skirt of the koshare doll.

"Oh, you know, way back. You know any of those

stories when those folks came up here from the Yucatán, that kind of stuff?"

"You mean real old times, them folk that came before New Mexico was even New Mexico—all just Mexico, I think. All Spanish. I dunno," she said, still fussing with the koshare doll. "I get them all mixed up. You know they marry into this family and that, some go into pueblos, others with Navajos, others marry Spanish. You go up to the old cemetery. You see some of them stones." She put down the doll and looked up. "Yeah, some of them stones got those six-pointed stars." She touched her index fingers and her thumbs together to make a triangle. "You know a triangle right side up and one upside-down. What do they call them stars?"

"Star of Davis," Grace said.

"Yeah, yeah, something like that, Star of Davis."

"Star of David," Jerry said softly.

"Yeah, maybe, maybe that's it. Sounds more right, doesn't it. Star of. David." Margaret nodded. Then she put her fingers to the side of her head and gave a little tap to her skull. "I'm trying to think. I recall having a koshare doll one time with one of them stars hanging off its neck. Think I traded it, though."

They chatted on for a few more minutes, and then Constanza said they had better be getting along.

"You come back now, Jerry. I promise I'll try and remember to talk more English." Margaret Santangel stood in the doorway and waved. She waved the way a baby might wave, deliberately and slowly opening and shutting her hand.

Jerry smiled and climbed in the truck. Constanza was driving now and she turned to Jerry with her hand on the ignition key. "'Spose you want to go to the cemetery now."

Jerry nodded. Then spoke. "I mean yes."

Chapter 16

❖❖❖

THE CEMETERY WAS at the crest of a hill, and even though the buffeting winds had blown off a good bit of the snow, many of the tombstones remained half buried in drifts.

"You get out and poke around," Constanza said. "I'm staying warm in here." She had put the truck in park and left the motor running.

Jerry began to walk around. It wasn't a large cemetery, but it did look old. The tombstones seemed worn thin from scouring winds and weather. Many of the names were so faint as to be unreadable. She saw markings, some understandable—a crucifix, the bowed head of what appeared to be the Virgin Mary—but time had erased all the features so completely it was as if a ghost holy woman hovered over the grave of someone named Lopez, so worn by time and weather that only the trace of a smile was left. But then there were more inscrutable ones. They were designs, but none that she recognized. Among the twenty to thirty gravestones of the names that could be read, it seemed that they all belonged to one or two families, perhaps three. The most prominent last names were Gomez and Begay and Lopez. Nothing that Jerry recognized. The first names were barely visible and only a few letters of the middle names had survived.

On one there was a face, but it was too round to be that of the Virgin. It had the contours of a baby's face, but again the features seemed to have been erased by time so that only a slightly blurred almost-smile remained. Jerry crouched down to see it better. She assumed it must have been carved to look like a cherub; perhaps a baby lay in this grave. She hoped not. That was too sad. She scraped away some of the snow and saw the dim imprint of what appeared to be wings. There was a cross beside the left wing. She blew off more snow. The clear outline of a triangle appeared by the right wing, and then upside-down and interlocked was another. A star!

"Aunt Constanza!" she yelled.

Constanza jolted awake. Good Lord! She never

dreamed the child had such a voice! She got out of the truck hoping Jerry hadn't wakened a rattler from its winter sleep and been bitten.

As she approached, she saw Jerry crouching by the stone. She had thrown her mitten down on the ground and was pointing with her finger at something inscribed on the tombstone. "What is this?"

"One of those Davis stars?" Constanza asked in a bewildered voice. "I mean Stars of David." Jerry nodded. "And a cross, and is that some kind of angel?"

Jerry nodded again and then spoke. "Who's buried here, Aunt Constanza?"

Constanza shook her head back and forth slowly. "I don't know. I don't know."

"Why do they have crosses and stars and angels all mixed up together?" Once again Constanza shook her head slowly.

Jerry looked around in frustration. "There are only a few names. Lopez, Begay, Gomez."

"There were some Begays in our family once, I think."

"But there aren't any Lunas—our name, Aunt Constanza."

"Oh, Luna was mostly used as a middle name for girls in our family."

"You mean it wasn't your last name?"

"Oh no, child. I think it died out as a last name way long ago. But you know the Spanish tradition is that you include a mother's last name by giving it as a middle name to your children. My mother was real keen on that. Both my sister, Jeraldine, and I had Luna for our middle name."

"But what was your last name?"

"Morillo."

"So why didn't you keep it?"

"Liked Luna better," Constanza said simply, and shrugged. "And see, isn't it nice that kind of by hook or by crook it got passed on down to you?"

"By hook or by crook," Jerry repeated.

"Come on, child. You're looking awfully cold. Let's go home."

Jerry picked up her mitten and got up. "Look at that hand of yours raw with cold. You'll be getting frostbite next thing. Then what good will you be to me?" Constanza grabbed Jerry's bare hand and held it to her mouth and blew hard on it.

Chapter 17

❧❧❧

"HELLO!" PADRE HERNANDEZ stepped out of his station wagon and waved as they turned into the drive. Jerry felt a terrible feeling in the pit of her stomach. Constanza switched off the ignition and gave her hat a fierce tug to set it firm against the wind that was kicking up whirls of snow devils outside. The wind whipped the black robes of the padre as he made his way toward the truck. Constanza and Jerry both got out. Jerry felt a compulsion to run inside and straight to the cellar.

"Jerry hasn't been to Mass and I was out in this direction and thought I'd stop in to see if everything's all right."

"Everything's fine," Constanza said.

"Jerry all right?" the padre pressed. Jerry nodded and began walking toward the house.

"She's just fine." Constanza hesitated. "She's just sorting things out. We all have to do that sometimes, you know." Then she began walking toward the house. "I'd invite you in, Padre, for a cup of tea. But there's a mess of orders to be straightened out."

"Yes, yes, of course. Didn't mean to intrude."

"It's never an intrusion, Padre," Constanza said warmly. "Just caught us at a busy time—orders, Easter coming up, lots of things to sort out."

Then she looked around at the mounds of snow in the yard. "Imagine this. Blizzard when spring should be around the corner. Well, you never know in New Mexico, do you?"

"Sure don't. But it never stays around that long. Sun could come out tomorrow and burn all this off," he said.

Jerry nearly tripped when she heard the word *burn*. Would she ever be able to hear that word again and think of it in a normal way? She just wanted to get inside—away from the padre, away from the whiteness of the snow-covered world. The cellar beckoned now like an old friend. The idea of the amber-tinged light, the dust, the smell of the earth, the sandstone, the spider that she only sometimes saw but whose presence had become a strange comfort—that was the place where she belonged. She wanted to think about the cemetery. She wanted to think about what her aunt had said about the name Luna and the Begays. Luna, she had said, was often used as a middle name. Luna was an old Spanish name. Miriam had married a man named de Luna. But Begay, she knew, was a Navajo name. It had nothing to do with the old world of Spain.

She stared down now at the lid of the trunk. SdL. She traced the intaglio of pinpricks with her finger. Sanchez de Luna. It was like a bolt of lightning had suddenly illuminated every dark wonder and dim question in her mind, and she knew now with absolute certainty that this was Miriam's trunk. Of course it was. There might be things from other people in it. But it was Miriam to whom this trunk first belonged. For only Miriam would have those exact initials, the ones of her maiden name and those of her married name. The trunk had been made for her. Jerry lifted the lid now and peered in. She had replaced the piece of lace and the letter and the medal. But she knew that there was another silver piece, most likely made by Beatriz's father. She felt her fingers touch something cold.

Hah! she thought. It was slender and blackened and cylindrical, a tubelike thing not more than three inches long. She wet her finger and rubbed. She could feel a design and, after a minute or so of rubbing, the tarnished black surface lightened to dark gray. One end was open and it looked as if it might have had a lid or stopper of some kind. It could have been for oil, or perhaps perfume. If there had been a scent, it had long since vanished. And yet in her mind another scent came back, a familiar scent. Jerry rested her elbows on the edge of the trunk and closed her eyes and tried to place the scent. She saw the red hat once again.

"Señorita Miriam," and with a flourish Don Solomon Ben Asher presented his hat into Miriam's hands. There was the faint scent of limes when he removed his hat. Reyna said it was an oil that he used on his hair.

"Miriam!" Jerry spoke the name aloud in the cellar. The sound seemed to swirl and merge with the scent of the limes. But this was a different Miriam. An unimaginably old Miriam, older than Doña Grazia, with more years than a century. A woman in whom the accretions of age had amassed like sediments of time from the beginnings of the earth. . . .

✦✦✦

In the House of the Apothecary
ON THE STREET OF THE NASRID
GRANADA, SPAIN
JANUARY 1492

✦✦✦

Esther

"Maria!" Mama keeps trying to wake up my great-grandmother. I don't know why they don't let this poor old lady rest. She doesn't want to be wheeled out here in her roll chair to see this stupid spectacle from the balcony. She told me so herself. But Papa and Mama feel that she must be stimulated. I think she is stimulated. I think she pretends to sleep. I think she does not want to see this parade, this triumphant march of the king and queen arriving in Granada.

"Abuela, you want to go out to the balcony and see the king and queen arrive?" Mama says this, and then turns to me. "Esther, don't you think Abuela wants to see the king and queen?"

"No, she doesn't," I answer fiercely. "What does she care? This is not such a wonderful moment. Look, they have already renamed the street. Did you see the sign go up yesterday?" It is now called the Calle de los Reyes Catolicos, Street of the Catholic Monarchs.

"Mama, will they rename our street?" my little brother Avraham asks.

"Who knows," she says, and then bursts out impatiently. "Oh, take her out there. The sun is out. She needs some fresh air."

Poor Abuela. I look at her. She is so ancient. She has over one hundred years. Mama says she is maybe one hundred and ten, but perhaps even older. They think she is so old that she doesn't care, or hear, or maybe even think. But she does. I know. She has told me that sometimes she pretends to sleep. She tells me that she doesn't talk because sometimes she doesn't want to tell people what she really thinks. And she does think. She told me that she hates her name. So now she has decided not to answer to it anymore. She talks to me of these things. She told me her real name. It was Miriam. Miriam Sanchez de Luna. De Luna is my middle name. It was the middle name of my grandmother Juana, who is now dead. So my mother gave it to me as my middle name. It pleased Miriam very much at the time. But now she thinks only about her first name. So I try to call her Miriam and told Mama and Papa and Avraham and the little ones and Luis to call her that, too. But they forget—all except for Luis.

Luis made Abuela's special chair when he came here more than ten years ago. My life changed when Luis came. For years we had lived freely here as Jews in Granada. Maybe Mama and Papa had heard rumors of what happened in other places, but they protected us. We didn't know. I think of those times and I think it was like living in a cocoon, all wrapped up and protected. But when Luis came, this cocoon of tranquility and safety was pierced momentarily. I shall never forget the day he came. He was no more than fourteen or fifteen. I knew he was special from the first. But he was strange. His eyes were too large for his face. It was as if he had seen too much, and he had. Mama gasped. "Brianda!" she said. "It is as if I am looking at Brianda." Brianda had been Luis's mother. I peeked out from behind Mama and saw his thin face, so pale that it appeared to me like a dim lantern in the dusk of our narrow street. Then he spoke. "My mother is dead, burned at the stake. My father is dead, burned at the stake. My sisters have been taken away. I have nowhere to go."

In the space of one minute my world changed. At first I didn't want to go near Luis. I felt that his parents' death clung to him like the pox. I thought I would catch it. I know it sounds stupid. But Luis too did not really want to come near us. He told me that he felt that he was a freak, so different that somehow his differentness would touch us in some horrible way. That he would spoil our perfect world. So Luis hardly spoke when he first came here. Gradually he spoke a little bit more, and over time, in bits and pieces, his story came out.

He had walked to Granada. That he had been able to thread his way through the inquisitorial police guards and leave Seville was a miracle; that he had walked all the way to Granada was unbelievable. Perhaps not. He seemed like a shadow of a child to all of us. So insubstantial as to be nearly invisible. The hollow look in his eyes, haunted by visions he could never express, he was more phantom than flesh and blood. But finally the hollowness began to leave his eyes. At first Luis could not grasp the safeness, the security of our beautiful city. He could not believe that Jews could go anywhere, practice openly their religion. He badgered Papa to teach him more Hebrew. Indeed he reveled in the Jewish traditions of our household. My papa's family, the Cardozos, had lived for generations in Granada and had never been forced to convert. When Luis told me how his family had given up the Catholic faith and returned to their old faith— begun to secretly practice Judaism—it seemed so bizarre and strange. They knew so little. They pieced together the traditions, but it was like a blanket with immense holes in it. It was unbelievable when he told us the story of his first Seder. He had never known what the fourth question was until my youngest brother, David, had spoken it in a clear voice: "On all other nights we eat either sitting or reclining, but why on this night do we recline?"

That was not all Luis learned. When my other grandmother, who is now dead, baked the bread for the Sabbath dinner, she always took a pinch of dough and threw it into the oven while murmuring a *brache*, a blessing. When he had asked what the blessing was about, she told him the story. She explained that the bread was offered to remember the destruction of the Temple in Jerusalem. The small piece of dough, about the size of an olive, was burned in the oven as a kind of sacrifice. "We diminish our joy," she said, "in memory of the destruction of the Temple."

Papa loved teaching Luis and not just about being Jewish. Papa said he had never seen such a quick mind as that of Luis, and he arranged for him to be apprenticed to our cousin Jacobo Cardozo, who was a court physician. But most important, Luis had impressed Yusuf Hassan, the court herbalist, who let him into the forbidden gardens of the Alhambra, where he cultivated his rare plants. Jacobo Cardozo said that Luis was the most extraordinary student he had ever had, and now Luis, who is barely twenty-four, has been called in to attend King Boabdil and the royal family. But here is the problem. King Boabdil and his Moors have been defeated by the imperial forces of Queen Isabella and King Ferdinand. And I can assure you that Luis shall never serve in the court of the monarchs who burned his parents.

"Abuela, can I touch your bald spot?"

"David!" Mama scolds.

But Abuela has wakened up. She blinks as if the sun is too strong. The little ones, Emmanuel and David, love to touch the bald patch on her head.

David tells her that it looks like a map he has seen in Papa's cousin Jacobo's house. Oh, now Jacobo is coming up to her to say something. She wrinkles her nose. He always eats lots of garlic. Poor Abuela out here on the balcony, hearing crowds cheer the monarchs she couldn't care less about, waves of garlic washing over her, David patting her bald spot, his fingers still sticky with candy—no wonder she pretends to sleep.

Oh well, as long as I am out here, I might as well watch with the others. I'll stand right beside Abuela and make sure she is all right. I bend down. "I am right behind you, Abuela Miriam," I whisper softly in her ear. A ghost smile passes over her face, perhaps for the ghost girl who had to die when she left Seville those long years ago.

Although our own house is on the Street of the Nasrid, we still have a good view of the main avenue by which the monarchs will make their entry into our city. It has been just two months since King Boabdil, the last ruler of the Nasrid dynasty of Moors, capitulated to the Spanish monarchs. Ours was the last Islamic stronghold in the kingdom of Spain. And now it has fallen. The Moors who practiced the religion of Islam were always our best friends. But they are no longer in power, so I wonder what will happen to us. My mama had to leave Toledo when she was a little girl on the day of her First Communion. Her whole family came here. It was one of the few safe places in Spain, and the royal family and the court promised it would always be safe in Granada. But it was a different king then. And Isabella was just a girl. Little girls change.

And cities will change. Our lovely Granada, perched on the edge of a beautiful valley, forever has insulated us from the ugliness of the rest of Spain, from the Inquisition, from the hatred. I am a spoiled rich girl. I know nothing of discomfort. I have never really feared, and now I fear coming out of this silken place I call a cocoon, this haven. I fear it terribly. I have seen nothing and yet in a sense I have seen it all—in the eyes of my dear cousin Luis. I am deeply in love with Luis and he with me. We had planned a life here, to be married in Granada, where I have lived my entire life. He was to be a physician in the court of King Boabdil. But all that is changing.

The crowd roars. I stand on my tiptoes to catch a glimpse of this queen. She is supposed to be very tiny, but they say she rides on a high throne placed within her carriage. My eyes flinch. There is a blinding dazzle of sunlight and gold. I glance down. What is Abuela clasping in her hand? Ah, the perfume vial that King Boabdil gave to Luis the time Luis treated him for the gout. Luis gave that to me. But Abuela had so loved the scent of the lime oil that I gave it to her. She keeps it in the small reticule that always hangs from her wrist. A dozen times a day she takes it out to sniff the scent.

There is another roar from the crowds. In the distance I can see the white horses of the monarchs, clad in their golden battle carapaces. What must Luis be thinking, feeling? To see once more the monarchs who had sent his mother and father to the stake. My beloved Luis! I must go stand beside him. I can see that his knuckles grip the rail of the balcony so hard they are white. I lace my arm through his. "I am here, Luis. I am here."

The queen passes by. Even from here we can see that the queen does not wear her years well. Stout and slightly bent, she raises a jeweled hand to wave at the throngs of people. The king looks much younger by comparison. Luis has been silent all this time. Then he speaks. "You see that man riding in the carriage behind the monarchs?"

"Yes," I say.

"That is the queen's confessor—Torquemado."

There is a thin smile on the man's face.

Luis's hand clasps my hand more tightly now. He begins to speak in a low voice. "It is Torquemado who tells the Muslims not to fear anything. He says that the queen gives them guarantees of full liberty to practice their religion. To protect their property and customs. He says that Ferdinand and Isabella took a solemn oath promising this. I don't believe it. The queen and king are weak and stupid. Torquemado will turn them, despite their oath." Luis's face has turned deathly pale.

"Are you all right?" I ask.

He turns his dear face to me. "Would I kill them if I could, Esther? Would I kill the queen, the king, and their confessor, Torquemado, who are responsible for my parents' deaths? I am a physician now. I am pledged through my oath to save lives at any cost. But I do hate." His nostrils pinch together and I know what he is thinking, no, not thinking, smelling. He told me about it once. I had begged him not long ago to tell me all about what had happened in Seville. I felt that I must somehow share his burden, the burden of his parents' deaths. So he told me about the stench of those fires sizzling with the flesh of his parents. How the stench of the burnings every day for more months than he could remember finally drove him from Seville. He ran not simply to save himself but to escape the terrible fumes of burning flesh.

"How in God's name do I heal myself of hatred, Esther? If it becomes like the life blood that courses through my veins, that pumps through my heart, how am I then any better than Torquemado?"

I cannot answer him. Then behind me I hear the clatter of a small object falling on the tile of the balcony and the sweet scent of lime oil fills the air. "Abuela!" I scream.

And then Abuela, in a very clear voice, almost that of a little girl, says a most peculiar thing. "Don Solomon! *Adecuado por . . .*" I do not even have time to wonder who this Don Solomon is, for the words die on my great-grandmother Miriam's lips as the lime-scented oil spills from the vial.

❧

Luis was right. No promises were kept, no guarantees respected. Indeed, my memory of our second-to-last night in Granada was not that of Luis's and my wedding held in the synagogue on the Street of the Jews, but of clapping my hands over David's ears as the voice of a town crier called out the news: Six Jews and two Conversos had confessed to performing an "act of conjuration" by tearing out the heart of a Christian child they had crucified on Good Friday a week past.

Blood libel. So now it had come to Granada. Luis had told me some stories that he had heard in Seville and other towns he had passed through years before, on his way to Granada. The most famous case had been the Holy Child of La Guardia. A body was never found. A child was never reported missing yet eight people were arrested, tried, and executed for a crime that never happened. It was all part of a strategy, Luis said. When it could not be proven that Conversos were secretly practicing Judaism, the officers of the Inquisition, the tribunals, began to spread myths about Jewish religious crimes, such as ritual murder or the desecration of the host. And these accusations had the added benefit of not just striking at the Conversos but the professed Jews as well.

The first story of blood libel in Granada was

made public on March 28. Two days later, on March 30, in the council chamber of the captured Alhambra, Queen Isabella and King Ferdinand signed the decree that drove into exile every Jew in Spain. We would have until the end of July to leave.

Now our family has been on the road for many days traveling west toward the frontier of Portugal. They say that there is no Inquisition in Portugal, that there are no tribunals. We must just pay a certain number of Portuguese *cruzados* for a tax and they will allow us to settle. I am tired of riding in the wagon next to Mama, who is still crying about Abuela Miriam. So sometimes I get out and walk. I cannot cry for her. I think she was an old lady of over one hundred years when she died. She had moved from Seville to Toledo, from Toledo to Granada—why in God's name should she have to move to Portugal?

"Will we be allowed to settle anywhere in the country, Luis?" I ask.

"So they say," Luis replies in a distracted manner.

We are approaching Guadalquivir River, the river that begins in Seville. I must keep talking. This part of our journey will be unbearably hard for my dear husband. Too many memories. Although it has been hard for us to leave Granada, I believe with every step it takes me and Luis away from a vile country and two demon monarchs to a better place. The glorious kingdom of Castille, the jewel of Spain, to me is an obscene place. If Luis and I are blessed with children, I would never want them born on Spanish soil.

We climb to the crest of a hill now. Below, the sinuous river flows into the port of Palos. All the wagons are stopping, for the view is grand. The sight in the harbor below us is an arresting one. Three ships with royal banners flying bob silently on their anchor cables.

"So that is the grand enterprise," Papa says as he walks over to us.

"Yes, the ships of Columbus." Luis sighs. "He saved my uncle's life."

"Who, Columbus?" Papa and I both say at once.

"Christopher Columbus. He seeks to sail to the Indies. My Uncle Tomás was released from prison after he was arrested with my father because he, along with Luis Santangel, the king's exchequer, had argued Columbus's cause to the king and queen and raised much of the money. And Tomás's daughter was to marry Santangel's son."

"So they seek a new world," Papa says softly.

"A new world to make filthy," I hiss.

The sound of tambourines swallows my words. It is the two rabbis who have been a half kilometer behind us. They refused our offer to ride in the wagons but insist on walking side by side with the people singing songs, chanting prayers, telling stories. Emmanuel and David have walked with them for several miles. I am suddenly ashamed of my bitter words. I must be like these two rabbis—cheerful and ready to encourage. I am a spoiled girl. There is no room nor time for spoiled girls now.

This world that I am leaving will begin to fade. Could there be some way of keeping the good parts and forgetting the bad? I will remember our Sabbath dinners, the light dwindling in the sky, my father's mother lighting the Shabbos candles. In the summer there was the smell of the wax swirled with the scent of the jasmine that blew in from our walled garden. I remember the first time that Abuelo Cardozo told me that some believed that the Sabbath came as a bride, a beautiful bride, dressed I then imagined in a gown of lace like the lace of my great-great-grandmother Doña Grazia Sanchez. And I shall of course remember always the splendor of the Alhambra, where we were sometimes invited by the court apothecary to come visit. There were the gardens, the pavilions, and the pools. But what had fascinated me the most was the filigreed stonework and plaster that made the palace and all the buildings seem as if they had been constructed from lace. I must think of these things now. They will take my mind away from the heat, the soreness of my feet, the tedium of this endless journey to Portugal. I remember how Papa would play a game with me and Avraham. We would stand in front of one of the stone walls that had been pierced to make a seeming infinity of designs—rosettes, entangled figures, a myriad of geometric shapes—and then he would ask us to find the patterns. It was like a treasure hunt. I was very good at it. Papa told me that I had a lace maker's eye, just like my great-great-grandmother Grazia Sanchez.

I have with me in the trunk that was once Abuela Miriam's some of the pieces of lace that Doña Grazia made so long ago in Seville. And in my pocket is the perfume vial. I run my fingers over the vial, and even without seeing find the patterns. I know the loveliness of the designs. How could God create a human mind capable of conceiving such subtle and intricate patterns and one that could invent as well the atrocities of blood libel? How for that matter could the Inquisition have been invented, the *quemaderos*, the machines of torture that I have heard rumors and whispers about that lurk in the dungeon prisons beneath the great cities like Seville and Toledo and Madrid?

I must stop walking for a second. The sun beats down on my head, through my scarf to that patch I always scratch. The sun feels like a hammer on an anvil that is my head. My bad habit, that patch! How long have the women in my family been doing this? How many have scratched themselves bald? I don't like to think about it. I press my hands to my eyes. Sunspots and little broken curly designs dance on the insides of my eyelids. A pattern . . . a pattern. I shall look for a pattern. In the trunk there is a small piece of lace, stained, but with a pattern like that of the scales of a dragonfly's wings. I close my eyes tighter and try to picture its delicate design. But suddenly I know that the stain is blood. It is blood and it is spreading. The lace is becoming drenched in blood. Blood lace, blood libel. The words swirl in my head. An inconceivable notion like a shadow crosses my mind: Is it possible that there is no God? Or worse, is it possible that God has simply left us, abandoned us on this dusty road? Has God really forsaken me? That is my last thought as I slowly crumple to the ground and breathe in the dust of the road.

Chapter 18

❖❖❖

IT WAS FRIDAY NIGHT. Jerry was dressing with care. She tied her hair back with a velvet ribbon and put on a pretty blouse that Constanza had bought her for Easter. She tucked it into some new gray wool slacks that she had bought on a recent shopping trip and thought were too nice to wear for school. There was a deep silence in the house. So deep that any little sound seemed to pop out with an exclamation mark. And what Jerry heard now was the rasp of a match being struck. Jerry paused. These were not Lenten candles. These were Shabbos candles, candles just like the ones Esther had watched her grandmother light in Granada. But Aunt Constanza didn't know this. Her aunt spoke the truth. She simply did not know. And who did know, for when a custom, a tradition, is cut off from its roots or practiced so long in secret, it begins to disintegrate. It becomes lost or turned into something it was never intended through some strange process of denial. Jerry imagined these things, these traditions like tattered remnants, unintelligible, or shattered pieces like fossils smashed on the desert of what once had been a rich faith, then picked up again, perhaps unrecognizable and patched into something else. A crazy quilt of faith and gods and ritual.

Constanza's back was facing her as she came into the kitchen. Outside the light was dwindling in the sky. She could smell the wax, the wax as it mingled with the sagebrush. How far had they come? Why do I know, Jerry thought, why she lights these candles, and she does not? Why do I know why she throws the piece of dough in the oven, and she does not? Why do I know that this time between time, this holy time that happens every seventh day and arrives like a mystical bride veiled in lace to be welcomed on the Sabbath day, is called Shabbos, and she does not?

The light drained from the sky, and the Sangre de Cristo Mountains—minutes before red and feverish—turned violet and then a dusky blue. The first stars pierced the sky as Jerry and Constanza sat down to the roast chicken.

Constanza looked out the window over the two flickering candles. "Ah, Estrellita." She sighed, and a look of utter peace settled upon her face.

"What?" Jerry asked aloud.

"Estrellita—'little star.' You know *estrella*, that is 'star' in Spanish, but these first stars are called *estrellitas*. My great-great-oh, so many greats-grandmother's name was Estrella. Lovely name. And when she was little, they sometimes called her Estrellita—little star. I liked that so much I had a dolly that I called Estrellita."

"Estrella?" Jerry spoke the name softly. "Was there ever anyone named Esther?"

Constanza looked momentarily confused. "I don't think so. Why would there be anyone named Esther?"

Should she tell her? There was so much to tell. Where to begin? She had no idea. "Well," Jerry said finally. "As you told Padre, I am sorting things out. And last night I found this."

"What's that?" Constanza squinted across the table.

"A vial, a perfume vial. It belonged to a girl named Esther, and her middle name was de Luna.

Esther de Luna Cardozo Perez."

"Yes, well, maybe Esther is close to Estrella. I told you," Constanza said, dishing out some blue corn and mashed potatoes. "Estrella's been a favorite middle name for many generations."

"Yes, many. Esther de Luna Cardozo lived in Spain, in Granada, until she left in 1492 when all the Jews were expelled." Constanza was holding the serving spoon midair, her eyes riveted on Jerry.

"Maybe your many great-greats-grandmother Estrellita was named for another great-great-grandmother named Esther," Jerry said.

"Are you trying to tell me that we're Jewish?"

"I'm not sure, Aunt. Does it bother you?"

"I don't know. It's just a shock. That's all. I mean, I thought I was a Roman Catholic. I was raised Catholic."

"I know. So was I."

"Confusing, isn't it?"

"Very," Jerry replied.

Chapter 19

❦

CONSTANZA LUNA STOOD over the sleeping form and watched the dim, flickering movements of Jerry's eyes under her lids. It was three hours past midnight. In another half an hour she would have to start the fires in the hornos, but she didn't know what to make of what Jerry had told her tonight. There were many things that were unexplainable to Constanza. Not everyone lit candles on Friday night, she knew that; but her own mother had, and not just during Lent. So she had just kept up the practice. And some things she did that might seem odd to others she just chalked up to superstition. There was some aunt on the Indian side of the family, which she guessed was the Morillo side, who had always done it, and she had just assumed it had come up from the Yucatán Peninsula. But she wasn't sure what Jerry was talking about here.

She knew Jerry often went to the cellar at night. That's where she got these things—the vial, the letter. She hadn't pried. She didn't need to. She knew what the child did down there. What she herself had only dared to do once—open the trunk. It was too peculiar. Her sister, Jeraldine Luna Morillo, who was much older, had the trunk up until she died. She had called it a hope chest. Hope chest! Of all things. But Jeraldine was a little bit off—everyone knew that. Nice but off. She had a crazy daughter, Elizabeth—Betty, they called her then. Betty had Mildred, and Mildred had Jerry. The minute Constanza had opened the trunk that one time years and years ago, she knew there wasn't anything like hope in it. Just awful musty things but each one with a kind of terrible dark little halo. She had picked up that same piece of old lace Jerry had shown her. She saw that stain—pale, brownish in color. She knew it was blood. Somebody's blood. There was violence in that trunk and dark secrets and she did not want to know them. Yet at the same time she had been fearful to throw out the trunk. Superstitious, perhaps? Was she just turning into an old bundle of superstitions? She threw pinches of bread in the oven, never swept the dirt out the door. Was her candle lighting just part of all that?

And then tonight Jerry tells her this thing about Jews in the family. Jews do things on Friday nights? News to her. She never knew, she never cared before Jerry came, and she could not answer Jerry for any of it except to say "just some old superstition." And superstition had no place in her faith. God was not a superstition. Constanza was a good Catholic. She had been baptized in the church. Had become a communicant when she was what, eight, nine years old? There was no room for superstition in a true believer. But the truth was that she was superstitious of that trunk and she had been so fearful of it that she had never touched it in years and years.

As she looked down at Jerry, from the corner of her eye she caught a glimpse of paper on the floor. She bent to pick it up. It appeared to be the corner of a map—a very old map. The map showed a landmass, or the fragment of a landmass, that vaguely resembled a horn that hooked into a sea—not a sea, a gulf, the Gulf of Mexico, and on the other side of the horn was the Pacific. The fragment of land that she was looking at was the Yucatán Peninsula. This is where her people had come from. This was where maybe Estrella had been born. This is from where, it was said, the old bread recipes came, the bakers of the family. The Yucatán bakers. Her great-grandmother had told her that. Constanza's hands began to tremble as she held the piece of paper. If the child can do it, why can't I?

Chapter 20

❖❖❖

JERRY IN HER SLEEP felt herself floating on that strange borderline at the edge of dreams. She felt a presence, familiar but unnameable, hovering at the edge of her dreams. And where was she? She thought she had been in the cellar. She had reached for that map. There was a hot salty wind, a stinging wind gritty with sand, swirling with a rank tidal smell . . . and there was a woman. The woman was tall and she looked so much like her aunt but so different. Young and dark, much darker than her aunt, with high, rounded cheekbones, a bony nose that flared ever so slightly at the nostrils, the blackest eyes, and a cascade of black hair. No bald spot! This was no daughter of the Sanchezes or the de Lunas or the Cardozos. This was a new woman in a new world.

Village of Quimpaco
YUCATÁN PENINSULA, MEXICO
NEW SPAIN
1540
✦✦✦

Zayana

It is not just words that I am running out of with
this foolish priest, it is patience. They told me that
if I agreed to have the child baptized, I could then
sell my bread to the Franciscan friars of the new
mission. They did not tell me that I had to name her
a name of their choosing. Leona de Luna—that is
her name. Named for her father, León, who died
three months before her birth. And Luna because
her father said that the women in his family often
had the middle name of Luna. Now they tell me I
must not name her that. I am standing here before
their font of holy water and they say that this name
will not do. I must name her the name of a saint.
What do I know of their Christian saints? The
priest says Marina is a lovely name, a name of the
Holy Virgin mother. There are too many Marinas
already. They are thicker than flies on a dead horse.

They all want to be Marina—why? Easy. Doña Marina—hardly a virgin, mistress of Cortés. My mother knew her. Her real name was Ximaca. Aztec like us. But now I must think fast. The padre is telling me again. If I want to sell my bread, I must do what he says, I suppose. How else will I put food in my little girl's stomach?

"Milagros."

"Milagros? But Doña Zayana, why Milagros?"

"Because she is a miracle. She was born in the middle of the plague. She lived. I lived. Is this not a miracle? Cannot a miracle be as wonderful as a saint?"

He scratches his chin. A soft smile begins to slither onto his face. "It is an interesting thought, Doña Zayana. Yes, I believe we can accept that."

Then I have a sudden thought. I remember León saying that if he had been a girl, his father would have named him Jerusalem. They were secret Jews back then in Portugal, and his father wanted to name a girl after the holy city of Israel. Why can I not have two names?

"Padre, I have thought of another name, a second name."

"Yes, Zayana. What might that be?"

"Jerusalem."

"Very interesting, Zayana. A child named for a miracle and the holiest of cities."

But for one named after a holy city and a miracle, little Jerusalem Milagros de Luna Perez is certainly screaming in a most unholy way. He now presses his thumb, which he has dipped in oil, on my little girl's forehead, then her chin and each cheek. She is turning bright red and screaming so loud. He speaks the priests' language. I do not know what the words mean. It is nothing like the Spanish I learned from León. I am to say "*sí*" to certain questions he asks me in Spanish. I do, but I don't pay attention, really. All I know is that the padre and I have a deal. He does this for me and I get to sell my bread to the mission. This has nothing to do with what they call religion. These men, these friars and priests, are so strange. They come with their god statues painted in milky colors with empty eyes and they burn ours. And they call our carved gods blazing with bright reds and purples "idols." Ours are not gods, are not sacred, so they say. Our gods have no power, so they say. And they wanted me to name my daughter after that white lady statue with her thin lips and empty eyes. How stupid. But our

Indian gods are so powerful that we would never dare name a child after one. It would be an insult, not an honor, to a god. Imagine me naming this shrieking red-faced baby after our feathered serpent god, Quetzecoatl. He is the god of twins and monsters; he is the god of the wind. Quetzecoatl descended to hell and retrieved human bones still dripping with blood and from them made a new race, our race. Aztecs. He has taught men science and discovered corn. His power is too strong for some little baby. She would die from the strength of the name alone. But I might make her a wind jewel from the shards of a conch like the one Quetzecoatl wore. That will be her talisman. That can protect her, more than the cross the friars and the padre wear. The wind jewel speaks of life, the cross only of death, the death of the god, the one they call Jesus Christ.

León's faith was that of the Hebrews. Had he lived longer, I would have learned more. I did learn some things. They worship only one god. They never show a picture of their god. León taught me to throw a small piece of bread into the oven before I bake. He told me that this was to remind the people of the destruction of the Temple in Jerusalem.

But now look at this, my little Jerusalem. She has stopped crying and she sleeps so peacefully in my arms. My Jerusalem! My Miracle!

❧ 1545

"Why do you do that, Mama?"

"Why do I do what?" I ask.

"Throw the little piece into the oven and let it burn up?"

"Because."

"Because why?"

"Because it was something your father taught me. It makes for good luck. "

Jerusalem touched the wind jewel that hung on a cord around her neck. "Like a charm—sort of?"

"Yes, like a charm. What a smart girl you are, Jerusalem Milagros de Luna Perez." She loves it when I call her by that long name. I bend down and pinch her cheek. "Now you go off and play. Where is your little friend?"

"Estrellita?"

"Yes, Estrellita."

"She is practicing the Credo so she can get a sweet from Padre."

"Oh, that's very good. Yes, when we deliver the

bread to the mission, I am sure Padre will be pleased."

"Yes, but she will have to share it with me because too much will give her a tummy ache."

"And have you practiced the Credo?"

"Oh yes, yes." Jerusalem began to hop around a mud puddle on one foot. The piece of conch shell, her wind jewel, bounced against her collarbone, and in a singsong voice she chanted the first lesson of the catechism.

"We Believe that the Roman Catholic Church is the One, True, Holy, Apostolic, and Universal Religion. Made by Our Lord Jesus Christ upon the Rock who is Peter and we believe in one Lord Jesus Christ, the son of God. . . ."

I watch her as she hops off toward the front door of our adobe. And I smile, then whisper to myself, "And I believe in doing business, bread business, and if they want to call God Jesus Christ and I want to call him Quetzecoatl, well, that's another kind of business altogether—private business."

❧ 1550

It is hard to believe that it has been ten years since Jerusalem was born and León died. Today is Jerusalem's birthday. I have taught her how to write

217

numbers, which I learned from León. And now she is with a stick writing the number ten in the dust of our cook yard, and with the ink I borrow from the padres, on the few scraps of paper I can get. Or she will write in charcoal from the spent fires. She is proud of her writing skills, especially today. She is, after all, the only kid in Quimpaco who can make figures, and I have taught her how to add and subtract. But I warn her about bragging. People don't like people who know too much. I, for example, I can read now. León taught me. But I keep it quiet. The padres would be disturbed and the village folk would think I was putting on airs. León taught me to read from his Bible. It is not like the padres' Bible. It does not have the part the padre tells us about in church—the Gospel stories.

But I do more figures these days than reading. I must keep my accounts for the bread. How much I sell, what I pay the miller for flour. Even Jerusalem is getting good at helping me keep these accounts. She's a smart kid. I thought Estrellita would go away when she turned ten years, but she hasn't. She still seems to be here. The imaginary friend comes around not quite so often but often enough. Elza, my sister, thinks it terrible that I indulge Jerusalem in this fantasy of hers. She tells Jerusalem that big girls don't have imaginary friends. But Jerusalem tells her right back, "Aunt Elza, Estrellita is not imaginary to me. She is imaginary to you." The other night Jerusalem told me that Estrellita is like one of the mysteries Padre talks about—things you can't really know or see but are still true. So you believe in them, she says—like the Trinity of the Father, the Son, and the Holy Ghost and the resurrection. It is the same with Estrellita. She is a mystery. "But Mama, don't worry; Estrellita is not a god. That would be blasphemous, right?" What do I know about blasphemy? "She's a kid like me. A lot like me. That's why I like her."

Today just as I am taking the last batch of bread out of the oven, the cart man from Quinque comes up the road. There is a large trunk in the cart.

"For me?" I call.

"For you, Zayana—all the way from Spain." I reach in my pocket to get out two *sueldos* to pay him. But my heart is thumping. From Spain. It is a trunk. Who could be sending me a trunk from Spain? León's parents. They must be long dead, I would think.

❧ ❧ ❧

"This is a very good sign, Jerusalem," I say. "Imagine this arriving on your birthday. There is no way he could have known."

"Who, Mama?"

"Your grandfather." I point to the wood placard that has been nailed to the trunk lid. *Luis Perez, Calle de Rosas, Lisbon, Portugal*, and there is another name on the trunk: *León Perez, Puerto Quimpaco*. But I do not understand why it is addressed to León. Did León's father not know his son had died ten years ago? I had the padre write to him about that and the birth of Jerusalem. Had the letter not been received? How awful that for all these years Luis Perez has not known that his son has been dead or that he has a granddaughter, Jerusalem. He knew of our marriage. For León had written him himself of that and we had received a reply with his father's blessing. León had said that he had done really what his father had wanted to do himself—come to the New World. Like his father, he had studied medicine. Then he had sailed to the Indies as a ship's doctor. First he had stayed in Hispaniola, and then went on to Cuba. The Indies were welcoming to people of "impure" blood, such as León, who had been forced to convert from

Judaism to Christianity. Although León told me that his own father and mother still practiced secretly their old faith. He stayed in Cuba for a few years and then came to the Yucatán, where the new governor of the territory had requested doctors and "men of learning."

But now after all these years, this trunk.

"Open it, Mama! Open it!" Jerusalem is dancing around me like a little sprite. But in truth I am almost afraid to open it. Surely there will be a letter inside and I hope I can read it. I cannot bear to think of taking it to the padre. "Open the trunk, Mama! Open the trunk!" Jerusalem is screeching now.

Every night for two nights I have bent over this letter, trying to take meaning from this thin, slanting script of my father-in-law, Luis Perez. I move my lips around the words and finally they begin to make sense. The words do indeed seem like something of a miracle. *My dear son, I hope this finds you and your wife well. Your mother, Esther*—Esther!

I had never known the name of León's mother. We had only been married for such a short time. We were young, and foolishly we thought we would have a lifetime to share stories and memories and little bits of information. But is it not a sign that Jerusalem's imaginary friend's name, Estrellita, is so close to the name of her grandmother!

I have some exciting news for you. You possibly remember my speaking of an uncle of mine, Tomás Mendez, who was very powerful in the court of Isabella and Ferdinand. Well, a grand-nephew of his has been appointed to a high post in the court in New Spain to govern a region called Nuevo León. His name is Julio de Luna, for indeed he married a de Luna from your mother's side of the family. So you are related to him from both sides, which is good! I hope that you will have the opportunity to seek him out. You yourself might want to travel to this new province, for I am sure they need good doctors. It pleases me to see our relatives going to the New World. If we were not so old, we too would come, but I rest now in the knowledge that our family is planting new seeds in this new world. And this brings me to explain about the trunk in which you found this letter.

As your mother and I approach our eighth decade of life, we feel the time has come to send

to you this trunk that has the bits and pieces of
our lives and the lives of your grandparents and
their parents and even their grandparents. The
trunk we think was originally the wedding chest
of your great-great-grandmother on your
mother's side, Miriam Sanchez de Luna, who
was born in Seville in the year 1381. It seems to
have come down through the generations of
women. I remember in the terrible year 1492,
when your mother and I joined the thousands of
exiles who left from Spain for Portugal, we took
in our wagon only two trunks, this one and
another that had our clothes and some crockery
and the instruments of my medical profession.
You perhaps remember this trunk, for it stood at
the foot of your mother's and my bed. There is
nothing of great monetary value in it. There are
a few silver pieces made by the husband of your
great-grandmother Beatriz, who was an
esteemed silversmith in Toledo. There is in fact
a mezuzah made by this same silversmith, which
I hope you shall put by your door as commanded
by the ancient biblical passage in Deuteronomy:
"And these words that I command you this day
shall be in your heart and you shall inscribe

them on the doorpost of your house."

By putting up this mezuzah in this new world, you will be able to do what we cannot do here since the Inquisition came to Portugal. You might touch the mezuzah and kiss your fingertips upon entering your home. And of course you must tell your wife and your servants never to sweep the dirt out a door when there is a mezuzah on its post.

I myself was surprised, indeed astonished, to find this mezuzah in the trunk. It would have been a dangerous object to possess; that someone had not thrown it away speaks greatly. You understand that it is not the money that these articles would fetch but the stories they hold: the dismay at what we have suffered and the wonder at what we have endured; the horror at what we have lost but the amazement at what we have held close. I can remember my first Seder, when not one of the men knew what all of the four questions to be asked were, and that when I finally came to your mother's house in Granada I learned all the questions. Yes, our faith and the faith of our fathers is in many ways like a tattered cloth, worn and threadbare *but still there. The Inquisition can keep killing us one moment and baptizing us the next, but there are those who in their hearts keep repeating the Shema—"Hear, O Israel, the Lord our God, the Lord is one. And you shall love the Lord your God with all your heart, with all your might. And these words which I command you this day shall be on your heart. You shall teach them to your children, and you shall speak of them when you sit at home."*

I must stop reading for a minute, for I am struck by how similar these words are to the Credo that the padres teach Jerusalem. This was a credo that is not perhaps so full of ghosts and mysteries, but it is a credo nonetheless and I like it! This credo speaks of only one God, one spirit, not the three of the Trinity; but even so I think this God could be a feathered serpent if I want it to be so. . . . It is a God without a face. That is good. "Jerusalem! Jerusalem! Come here!"

"What is it, Mama?"

"I want to teach you something. Everyone should learn something new when they turn ten."

Then Jerusalem Milagros de Luna Perez turned

to the air beside her and said in a hushed voice, "Listen carefully, Estrellita."

Later that same evening, when Jerusalem is sound asleep and her soft breathing purrs through the air of the adobe, I fetch a candle and get out León's Bible and open it to the Book of Deuteronomy. Some of the verses sound very much like the Credo, for there is the commandment to love the one God and to teach the children. The words are almost identical. I close the book. And begin to think. There are too many good signs to ignore. The name of the province itself is the same as that of my beloved husband, León. His mother was named Esther—so close to the imaginary friend of Jerusalem. The relative in the province was named de Luna, the moon! The signs are all there.

I must walk to Nuevo León. I must meet my husband's relations. I must begin a new life. I shall find work—I am after all a baker. This is my credo!

I get up and walk into the yard and take a pinch of dough and throw it into the oven as I do every morning between the last of the evening stars and the first light of the new morning. But this is the last time I shall do it here in Quimpaco. The thought excites me. Tomorrow we shall leave! I go in and look at Jerusalem. I am so excited I almost want to wake her up to tell her of our great adventure. But she sleeps with the wind jewel clutched in her right hand as she often does after she takes it off in the evening.

Chapter 21

✦✦✦

WHEN JERRY WOKE up the next morning, she touched the shell at her neck. The wind jewel. Could this be the same one? Jerusalem's wind jewel? She had taken to wearing it all the time. Usually she took it off and put it by her bedside table. Last night, however, she'd forgotten. But she looked now at the table. The paper, the map fragment had been moved! If it had fallen onto the floor, she could have understood. That would have seemed natural, but the paper had moved from one side of the table to another, and its corner was under the small mat on which her reading lamp stood. That could not be accidental. Someone must have moved it. Someone? There was only one other person in this house. Then she recalled the presence that she had sensed hovering over her as she had slept, the unnameable presence at the edge of her dreams. Constanza! But it was not simply that Constanza had come into her room. She had in some way entered Jerry's dreams. Jerry began to tremble. It had been so easy when everything was neatly divided between the world up here and the one down in the cellar. But now these two worlds were not just overlapping; they were beginning to penetrate each other.

"Baked goods always do lousy during Lent," Constanza growled as she, Jerry, and Sinta drove up to the church. This was to be Jerry's first time at the church in weeks. But she was not coming for a service. It was the church fair and the weather was fine, so most likely it would be held outside. Jerry and Sinta had agreed to help at the fair—run the pinto bean toss for the children. In exchange Sister Evangelina promised them first pick, if they came early, from the Saints' Closet, the name of the donated clothing section.

"There's not going to be anything good," Sinta said.

"I found a pair of work boots last year," Constanza said.

"I mean fashion," Sinta said.

"Of course there's no fashion. Have you ever seen anyone fashionable in this church? I haven't, and I've been coming here for over fifty years." Ahead a station wagon lurched into the church driveway and there was a grinding of gears. "Oh, good Lord, we should all be buying crash helmets. It's Sister Evangelina," Constanza muttered.

"Hi, girls—my angels of the pinto toss! Okay, a deal's a deal! Go right to the Saints' Closet and take your pick."

Sinta had been right. There was nothing worth looking at on the rack. Sinta had gone over and begun to pick through a bin with odd bits of jewelry. "Look, this is sort of cool." She held up a zebra-striped hair clip.

"Nice," Jerry said. She walked over to the bin and began picking through.

"What's this?" Sinta said, holding up a tarnished silver cylinder. Jerry inhaled sharply. She knew what it was immediately. It was a mezuzah. Sinta turned it over in her hands. "Look at these designs on it— weird."

"It's Hebrew."

"Hebrew? How do you know?"

"Because."

"Because why?"

"Just because." Jerry shut her eyes for a moment. Hadn't she had this conversation before?

"Are you all right, Jerry? I'm sorry. I'm really sorry. I shouldn't have pressed you. You've just been doing so well with . . . uh . . . the talking."

Jerry's eyes were still clamped shut. These two worlds were coming too close together. But she knew that she couldn't give up the one of the cellar. To do so would be to retreat again into a terrible silence; she just knew it. But she was scared. What was happening?

She took a deep breath and forced the words out. "That thing with the Hebrew, it's like a charm, sort of." She touched her sweater and felt beneath it the wind jewel. In that moment she knew her name was not Jeraldine, but that she was Jerusalem.

Jerry couldn't wait to get home. She had bought the mezuzah for ten cents from the Saints' Closet. She wanted to look at it more carefully. One end of the silver tube was smashed and the silver seemed to have thinned, and she wondered, if indeed she could pry it open, would she find the pieces of parchment with the words from Deuteronomy or other Bible passages? She was tempted to try and open it. But would this be considered sacrilegious?

In the cellar she stared at the mezuzah that she held. She had a sudden inexorable urge to pry open the thin end. She took a bobby pin from her hair. The tip was just right to insert. A minuscule piece of silver flaked off. There was something inside! She needed tweezers, a pin, anything. Did she dare go back upstairs? Constanza had gone to bed early, but perhaps she had not been asleep long enough to be really sound asleep. She had another idea. She bit off the rubber tip from the end of the bobby pin. That made it slimmer. She began to reinsert it. Perfect. Working carefully for several minutes, she finally extracted a darkened fragment of paper. Would it be the ancient biblical passage . . . *These words I command you this day*. . . . No! What was this Spanish word that jumped out at her: *limpieza*. . . . Jerry broke out in a sweat. There was something very wrong here.

But it did connect. There was a terrible, chilling connection between this fragment of paper and, yes, another fragment in the trunk. She had seen it. As if in a trance she lifted the lid to the trunk. She knew exactly where that fragment was. Like iron filings drawn to a magnet, her hand moved toward it. Jerry fitted the two fragments of paper together. It was still not whole but there was enough—and this was no biblical passage. *"Este documento verifica que el portador Julio de Luna es el cuarto descendiente de la generación de Cristianos puros sin la ascendencia judía descubrido por los cientos años pasados y por lo tanto esta concedido un certificado de la limpieza de sangre. . . ."*

Jerry slowly translated the words. It didn't matter that they were Old Spanish, that they were stained and sometimes a tear broke them up. The meaning of the words, like coils of hatred, descended into her consciousness and became clear. "This document verifies that bearer Julio de Luna is the fourth-generation offspring of pure Christians with no Jewish ancestry traceable for the last one hundred years and therefore is granted a certificate of pure blood with all the attendant rights and privileges and therefore is fit to hold public offices or any benefice within the Kingdom of Castille, and within its jurisdiction."

Jerry closed her eyes. "I remember," she whispered into the amber darkness. "I remember how Beatriz hated that word *limpieza*! How she said the word had been ruined. Blood . . . blood . . . clean blood . . . pure . . . blood . . . blood libel . . . blood secrets . . ." Jerry spoke, and as she spoke her voice seemed to fill the cellar and the amber light swirled about her. I am just a small particle, a dust mote in this history, she thought, and she saw a house, a wooden and adobe house on a street. There was a woman who looked so much like Constanza now, almost as old, it would seem. And there were secrets in the house—blood secrets.

The Merchant's House
THE STREET OF HERNÁN CORTÉS
MEXICO CITY
1590
❖❖❖
Zayana

I stole the *limpieza de sangre* when we first arrived in Tampico in the village of Pánuco. That bitch Dora. To think of the hopes I came with and how within a blink she dashed them all! But that was forty years ago, why am I thinking of that now? Ah, yes, I know. I know . . . I don't forget. I just lose the thread. Well, what can I expect? I am over eighty now. So the thread, why I am thinking of that stupid *limpieza*? Because when I first came here so full of hope with my darling little Jerusalem, I remembered my father-in law's words:

"By putting up this mezuzah in this new world, you will be able to do what we cannot do here since the Inquisition came to Portugal. You might touch the mezuzah and kiss your fingertips upon entering your home."

I thought I would do that. I liked the idea, and so when they led me to the little lean-to out in the backyard, not far from where they dumped the night soil, I might add, I thought, Well, I can nail this to our doorpost. It is the perfect way to honor my dear León's family. I forgot the other part of the letter, the part where León's father had written that it was a dangerous object to possess. It still was dangerous. I remember how hot it was that day. There is no hotter place than Tampico in late August. Humid, and mosquitoes so thick you kept your mouth shut and breathed only through your nose. It doesn't seem forty years ago. I can still hear her shriek.

"What are you doing? That is private property. You are to rent it from us for five *reales* a month. You do not have permission to nail up anything. What is that thing?"

"It came from Luis Perez, León's father. It has some holy texts from the Bible," I began to explain, and her face seemed to turn to stone.

Then she spat out the words. "We are not Jews. There are no Jews in this family. You stay right here. Don't move." I was scared. I could not imagine what she was going to do, but when she came back she held out a certificate. "I don't suppose you read, but I'll read this to you." I said I did read, but she paid me no heed. It was a fancy paper with a wax seal. She called it a *"Limpieza de Sangre."* After she had finished reading it, she drew herself up very tall. "You see. We are of pure blood and this is legal proof. How could we be Jews? We have a son named Jesús, and another in Spain studies for the priesthood. My great-uncle's second cousin was an archbishop. We are *hidalgos!* We are aristocrats and you never forget it. You foolish, stupid Indian. If you plan to stay here, we shall have none of that."

She treated me like donkey dung. She ripped the mezuzah from my hand and threw it as far as she could over the courtyard wall. In those days there was not even a street in this village, and on the other side of the wall it was the swamp. I was so angry I could have strangled her right there—this plump, pale woman with a face like kneaded dough and two small eyes set in it like tiny raisins. I vowed that I would find that mezuzah. The rainy times would not come for another two weeks, so there was still a chance. Every day I went out and searched. I prayed, too. I prayed to all the gods, the god of my husband, to Quetzecoatl and Atlau. I figured I needed all the help I could get. I even prayed to Jesus and the Madonna. My reasoning was that if these gods are truly powerful, if they are good, they must see what Dora did was evil—the way she spoke to me, the way she denied her own blood. The words that were written in the mezuzah were not bad words—what could be better than admonishing parents to teach their children to love something greater than themselves? Here was my reasoning for calling all the gods. I figured that God could be called one thing in one language or by one people and another name by another people. It still really was all one God, more or less. That is what I believed then and still believe now.

So every day and sometimes in the evenings, I went out to look for the mezuzah. And, in fact, four days before the rains came, I found it. It was near noon and I noticed a fierce glint in the weeds. There it was. It was as if it had been waiting for me. I was so happy, but I knew that I couldn't keep it on my doorpost. I tried to think where it would be the safest. Then I knew! It was an astounding thought. I would put it in the Madonna statue that Dora kept in the front courtyard and kissed every time she and her husband, Don Julio, and their children came home. And I too can touch the Madonna, then kiss my fingertips just as León's father did, but I shall know the truth of what's inside. What a trick, I thought, what a magnificent trick. So I got up when the house slept and I stole into the courtyard. As I thought, the Madonna was hollow and perched on a pedestal. She was a small statue and not heavy. So I just tipped her slightly and slipped the mezuzah inside into the folds of her gown. It was right where her ankle would be if the artisan had bothered to make her with legs, which he did not. Her weight rested on the hem of her gown. I nearly laughed out loud. Oh, how I delighted when I would see Doña Dora kissing that statue. If she knew!

Doña Dora proved impossible to live with. She treated me and little Jerusalem terribly. If she thought the taint of Jewish blood was shameful, she thought Indian blood just as bad and my little Jerusalem resembled me more than she did her father, although she did have his chin. But her skin was dark and her eyes even darker. Don Julio was not a bad man, but his wife gave him no peace. I was trying to do my baking, but I realized Jerusalem and I could not remain there. I began to look for another place to live, and shortly before we moved out, something very bad happened. Doña Dora was always very particular about her clothes, and she accused a serving girl of scorching one of her silk gowns. The girl was no more than twelve and she beat her so brutally that the child will be blind in one eye forever. I could not move out of this house fast enough. When would she turn on my little Jerusalem Milagros? Jerusalem, who had survived the plague, might not survive this woman with her raisin eyes and rancid breath. Yes, her breath was terrible. I don't know how Don Julio could stand to lie with her. I wanted to hurt her terribly. I wanted to scare her. I wanted vengeance for the serving girl and, yes, myself and all the other people she had hurt in life. The afternoon before I left, there was a sign that came to me. I was washing clothes in the stream when I heard a great beating of wings. Jerusalem looked up and said, "Mama, *águila*! *Águila!*" An immense eagle had landed on a rock on the other side of the stream. But I knew that this was not simply an eagle. No! It was Huitzilopochtli, the Aztec god of war and of the sun. The Aztecs believed that the sun god needed daily "nourishment"—*tlaxcaltiliztli*, that is, human blood and hearts. The hearts were offered on the sacrificial stone. I had heard about these sacrifices and so had Jerusalem, for she began to tremble fiercely as she too remembered who the eagle really was. She had heard the stories of the young virgins sacrificed. "Mama," she whispered. "Has he come for me?"

"No! Never. It is not your blood he wants. . . ."

And that was when I knew the true meaning of the eagle's presence. He did not want our blood. He wanted the pure blood. The blood of a *hidalgo*. He wanted the coveted blood of Doña Dora proven and certified by the fancy parchment in the gilt frame. I knew exactly how I would do it. The next night was to be my last night in the house of the de Lunas. I had already planned to go to the statue and retrieve the mezuzah, but now in its place I would leave the scraps of the *Limpieza de Sangre*. Yes, I would tear it up and hide it in the statue of the Virgin. This would destroy Doña Dora. And as a relic of my conquest, I would take one small scrap of the document with me. But it was not just a sign of my conquest. I had already taught Jerusalem the passages from the Bible that were in the silver vial, and now I would teach her a new thing. I would show her these little scraps of paper with the words at the top, *"El Certificado del Limpieza de Sangre"*; and my lesson would be, You can have the purest blood, but with a bad heart, it is worth nothing.

So why am I thinking of all this now. Jerusalem, my dear Jerusalem, she died so long ago, nearly thirty-five years ago with the birth of her child, Estrella. Yes, that is what she named her, after her little imaginary friend, Estrellita. And now I am an old lady and Estrella has married Carlos de Gusmao. He is a successful merchant. He deals mostly in tools for miners. It is a good business. Everyone wants to dig for gold here. He makes a nice living. They keep me well. This is how wealthy I am: I direct others now to make the bread. Although sometimes I do it myself, and yes, I still throw in the little piece of dough first for the Temple in Jerusalem. But now I also do it for

Huitzilopochtli. He is my good-luck god. Without him, I am not sure if I would have so successfully left Doña Dora, or if Jerusalem would have found such a nice husband; and though God took her, look what he left for me in my old age. Estrella. Estrella and Carlos are both secret Jews here in Mexico City, and tonight they come to me and they ask for that old mezuzah. So that is why I think all these thoughts from long ago. They want to put it someplace secret in the house, even if it cannot be on their front door. And I say no, let's get ourselves a nice Madonna. Go, Carlos, to the Calle des Artisans and have the man named Pedro make you a ceramic Madonna. I will show you how to put a mezuzah in her foot, or perhaps the skirt or her dress, and then you can kiss her every time you enter the courtyard and we shall all be safe.

They think I am a little crazy, of course, because I still throw a piece of the dough in for the old Temple in Jerusalem and one as well for my Aztec god, but they listen. You see, the Inquisition has come here to Mexico. Everyone said it never would, but it did. Oh, my goodness, did it come! Almost to our old doorstep in Tampico. So many who had come there to settle were in fact secret Jews. Not the awful Dora, but here is perhaps a trick worse than mine that the fates played on that woman—her husband, Julio, was! The *limpieza* wouldn't have helped him. The Holy Office paid no attention to such certificates. There were hundreds, maybe thousands of arrests and burnings—auto-da-fés, as they call them. So many that the province once called *Nuevo León* was renamed *El Quarto Tragico*, the Tragic Square.

But Jerusalem and I and her young husband, Rodrigo Benevista, had long left and come to Mexico City. Rodrigo's grandfather was rumored to be a rabbi in the old world, but Rodrigo's brother had been sent to study to be a Catholic priest and had just come to Mexico City. That is why we came here. Many years ago when we first arrived, things weren't so bad here in Mexico City. The Holy Office of the Inquisition mostly went after bigamists and blasphemers. But now they go after Jews. That is why I am frightened for Estrella and Carlos. It is this Jewish thing. They want to follow the laws of Moses. There are many Jews here in Mexico City. They call them Marranos. They go to their Friday night Sabbaths in the cellars of their friends. Each time I worry so. I cannot fall asleep until they return. And now especially with the baby coming. If it is a girl, they want to name her Jerusalem de Luna. A nice long name, Jerusalem de Luna Perez de Gusmao.

❧ *A few months later*

Estrella of course had to wait until our two servants left for the day. One was so old she would not have noticed, but the other was young with sharp eyes. And now it was more important than ever not to arouse their suspicions. Too many people were being arrested. I was nervous. We had heard that as many as fifty had been carted off in the last month, and these were not bigamists or blasphemers or brigands. No, they were people suspected of being secret Jews because they had been reported by a neighbor or more often a servant for such activities as wearing fancier clothes on Saturdays, cleaning their houses on Fridays, or most telling of all, lighting candles on Fridays when it was still early and not yet dark—all signs of observing the Jewish Sabbath. Another sign of the secret Jew was if a fire was not lit after sunset on Friday and kept cold all day Saturday, for the laws of Moses did indeed forbid such kindling. Now the Holy Office had posted an *annuncio* listing such suspicious activities. Handsome rewards were given for reporting people.

So Estrella and Carlos pieced their little Sabbaths together as best they could. I kept watch for them sometimes and even lit the fires. As I told Estrella and Carlos, I am not really a Jew, so there was no problem for me to light the stove after the Sabbath began. It has been rumored that the tower that was built new for the church was so officers of the Inquisition and their spies could go up on Fridays and Saturdays to see from which houses no smoke rose. Those smokeless houses were immediately suspected of being the homes of secret Jews.

For Estrella, I admit, it must be hard to tell what God I follow. Sometimes within one sentence I might invoke the name of three gods—Adonai, the Hebrew name for the one God; Huitzilopochtli, for that's my own private Aztec patron saint; and sometimes I have even been known to call upon the Blessed Virgin, who has after all protected the mezuzah for me all those years, starting when Estrella's mother and I had lived in Tampico. Carlos sure did squirm when I had suggested that if he wanted to keep a mezuzah here, he put it into a Virgin statue.

But I understood. Carlos and Estrella were trying so hard to live by the laws of Moses. But all they really had to go by were fragments. That's the way it is with most of the secret Jews around here. It has been so long since they have openly practiced their religion that only a few knew the ways, the prayers. All they have are bits and pieces now. Bits and pieces. They do know the Shema. And to think they had learned it because of the letter in the trunk that had come from her great-grandfather Luis, that trunk that I dragged all the way from the Yucatán to Tampico to Mexico City. The same trunk that had the mezuzah and God knows what else in it—pieces of lace, a tarnished medal of some sort. Oh yes, and now the baby cap that little Jerusalem has already outgrown. Tonight is their night to host the Sabbath. Not many will come. That would be too dangerous—just three or four, and they will of course go to the cellar.

The sun is setting now. Within minutes it will disappear. "Abuela!"

"Sí, Estrella." Time for me to go hold the baby. It's this way every Friday night ever since Estrella has discovered the ritual of welcoming the Sabbath. She learned about this from her friend Ruth. It was

Ruth who had told her that one welcomed the Sabbath like a new bride on her wedding day. In the trunk Estrella has found several pieces of lace. Some were old and tattered, but there was one that although yellow with age looked like a fine net in which six butterflies had been caught. Estrella for some reason loves the old thing. She said that she felt drawn to it—a kinship with the woman who had worn it. Sometimes I think that maybe it had belonged to my mother-in-law, the one that had been called Esther.

The baby is asleep when Estrella places her in my arms. She is a beautiful child. And so is the mother. I watch as she puts the veil on her head and takes the two candles and the flint box and begins to walk down the earthen steps to the cellar. With each step down the stairs, I know that Estrella's spirits rise. She told me once that it is almost as if she can feel the delicate wings of the butterflies stirring the air around her head. For these brief moments she is indeed a radiant bride.

I am thinking about her striking the flint box to light the candles. Before the baby came, I would sometimes go down and watch this Sabbath ritual. She must be about to light the second one now. I like imagining the little lick of flame. It reminds me of León, for some reason. It connects me with him. What is that thumping outside my door? Why is my door splitting open? I open my mouth to ask who's there and only a terrible scream breaks from my lungs. It is the officers of the Holy Inquisition. I imagine those candles below in the cellar, the sizzle of the flame grabbing the wick, and then I know my entire world is about to change; the world of my Estrella is set afire.

❧ Six months later

So this is the second time I have stolen in my life. The first was the *Limpieza de Sangre* and now I steal my own blood back. Yes, Estrella sits like a stone beside me on the wagon cart. She wears a nun's habit and so do I. She hears nothing. She speaks not a word, and her eyes are too large for her head because they have indeed seen too much. She is filled up with horror after six months in the dungeons of the Holy Office of the Inquisition. They tortured her every day. They put her on the rack and they would stretch and stretch her. Now her one arm hangs loose out of its socket. She cannot hold her own baby. They brought her from the dungeon on the day of the auto-da-fé when they burned Carlos. They put her right up front so she could see him burn. I was there too, in the crowd. It is easy for an old Indian woman to blend in. You see, when they came to the house that evening, they barely paid me heed. They assumed I was a slave—so dark with that red tint in my skin, rocking a baby. As soon as I saw what was happening, I knew what I must do—play the ignorant servant. And Estrella then seemed to know too. She did not cry "Abuela" as they dragged her from the cellar. They had already arrested Carlos. I disappeared into the streets with the baby. I had money. I have always been good with money. They took the house. They took the business. How would the Holy Office exist if it wasn't from the treasures they plundered from the Jews? The bigamists and the blasphemers and the thieves give them nothing. That is why they turned on the Jews. They did not take the trunk, however. They opened it, rooted through it with their filthy hands, and found nothing of value. The veil of butterflies, however, was lost. They threw it in the fire.

It took me several days to find out where they had taken Estrella. The Inquisition is so secretive.

They don't use the regular prisons. No, they have dungeons under certain buildings. But I found out. And you can bet that the Holy Office is not the only ones with spies. There is an entire network of spies to help those inside and, yes, a black market too. You have to bribe guards to take messages in and bring word out, to take a loaf of bread, a rag for a woman's monthlies, whatever. I went back to baking. Yes, I'm an old lady, but anger brought me new energy. Energy I never knew I had. And I had one goal: get Estrella out of prison. Make a deal with the nuns and then steal her from their convent. I had money that León had left for me; I had used only part of it to go to Tampico. And then the money from my baking business. I had always saved it out, separate from Carlos's. I didn't even keep very much of it in the house on Cortés Street. I had other places. I started baking again when Estrella and Carlos were arrested. I made it a point to bake for the Dominican friars—the dogs of God, as some call them. I watched them very carefully. I knew that some of the friars indeed took bribes from secret Jews to keep the Holy Office from these Jews' doors. I just had to figure out which ones. It was through a miner who had often bought tools from Carlos that I found out about one Friar Pascal. He liked gold, and since he could not exactly leave his order to go off and mine for gold, he found other ways to collect it. He was leaning heavily on Simon Levi. So I started watching. I wanted to catch him collecting the gold, then I could threaten to tell his superior and this might be enough to boot him out to the loneliest province. But I actually caught him at something better: He had a mistress and two children!

So now I confronted this so-called holy man, man of God. And this was the second time I made a deal with friars. The first was at the baptism of Jerusalem, so I could sell my bread. But now I am getting back my granddaughter, and once again it has nothing to do with what is called religion. It's a deal, that's all. There was nothing the friar could do for Carlos. Carlos would burn, but he could save Estrella if she agreed to be baptized and go to the nuns of Sancta Cordera. Fine. It's a deal, and to myself I think this is very good. Sancta Cordera is not far from the road north—north to the country known as New Mexico—and when the time is right, I shall steal back my own granddaughter.

✢ ✢ ✢

I stole her this morning with the help of the miner. She was out in the convent's field picking the corn. She can only use her one hand, of course, so she is quite slow. The other nuns leave her alone because she never talks and just stares, but I watch from the edge of a grove of trees. I had a friend sew me a nun's habit. It is so simple. I begin working in the field near to Estrella, because there are fifteen or so other nuns out there and they do not notice me. I edge my way over to Estrella. I begin working beside her. She pays no attention. It is as if the very air around her has turned to glass and she is sealed off. She is neither living nor dead—but apart and far away. Finally I take the mezuzah from deep within the folds of my gown. I take her good arm and whisper to her, "Look, look, this is what your Carlos died for. Did he not say the Shema as he burned? There is your child, your baby, Jerusalem, in a cart waiting to be taught."

We don't have a lot of time. The other sisters are drawing nearer as they work the rows of corn. If I could only remember the words, the words, but they have slipped from my mind—the words of Deuteronomy. Then suddenly the wind stirs, huge drafts of air churn overhead, and I see the nuns all

stopping in their work to look up. "*Águila! Águila!*"
The nuns are all crying out and they are ready to
cower, for indeed the eagle starts to swoop down on
them. Its talons extended, its craw opened in a terrible screech. It is my Huitzilopochtli! And with
him come the words of the passage: "*And these
words which I command you this day shall be on your
heart and you shall inscribe them on the doorpost of
your house.*"

And while those stupid nuns are squealing like
stuck pigs, I begin to whisper the words to Estrella.
And although her eyes remain large, she takes my
hand and I lead her into the grove where the cart
and her baby wait.

For two days now we have been traveling and still
she sits like a stone and says nothing. She barely
moves except to sometimes raise her good arm and
rub the place on her head where they poured the
holy water. I try to talk to her a little bit. I don't
push. I'm not a talky sort myself. But I try to tell her
when she pats her head, "Don't mind, Estrella . . .
what's a little holy water to a Jew? You are a real Jew
like your husband and your father and your grandfather and his grandfather."

I am not sure what I am. I am not sure if it really

matters for me. But I will put the mezuzah on our doorpost; no more hiding it in the Madonna's skirts. No, that is why we are heading north. And when we get there, I must remember my own father-in-law's admonition to never sweep the dirt out a door on which a mezuzah is nailed. Yes, I must remember that. And I must remember to look for the eagle in this new place. I am sure it will be there. But there are no deals to be made with eagles, of that much I am sure.

❖ New Mexico

"The last nail!" I announce loudly. "The mezuzah is up." I look around to Estrella, but she sits numbly in the chair in a spot of sunlight that has poked in through the door. A cool breeze blows. Jerusalem, who began to take her first steps shortly after we arrived, toddles across the dusty yard to me. Tomorrow the other settlers, well, at least four, have promised to come and help me build my hornos for baking bread. "All right, Jerusalem, let's you and me get Mama up from her chair and help her look at this—the mezuzah."

I keep thinking maybe it will make a difference. She still has not spoken a word since I fetched her from the nuns. She still stares with her huge eyes.

Even her baby cannot make her smile or blink or anything. Her arm never healed properly. Still, every night I put Jerusalem into her mama's lap and carefully wrap Estrella's arms around the chubby body of her daughter. I can't give up. I just can't. If I give up, it means they've won. I won't let them win. They have destroyed too many lives. But as Jerusalem grows bigger, she grows stronger, and she gets bored being held by the mama who is not quite alive. She begins to wiggle. Estrella's arms simply go limp.

A neighbor made a doll out of a corncob and sewed a bright dress on it for Jerusalem to play with. But little Jerusalem has no interest in dolls. Now I look over at Estrella just before I try to lead her to see the mezuzah. I am amazed. Jerusalem must have dropped the doll in her mama's lap and Estrella is sitting with the doll. In fact, I hear a muffled humming sound deep in her throat. It is as if a lullaby has lain buried inside her. This gives me hope. Estrella holds the little corn doll all day and all night.

❦ *A month later*

For weeks now Estrella has held the corn doll. But she rarely touches her own child and she never speaks. I think she might never speak again. I have not given up hope, but I now place my hopes in another—in Jerusalem de Luna Perez de Gusmao. This is life.

Chapter 22

❖❖❖

"JUST IN TIME, wouldn't you know it." Constanza leaned toward the kitchen window and squinted. "Sister Evangelina arriving just as the first batch comes out of the oven."

The kitchen swirled with the scent of the freshly baked hot-cross buns. Sinta and Jerry stood ready with their pastry bags to decorate them. They had been practicing on parchment paper. Constanza did not settle for a simple cross on the buns. On many she made a lily with delicately curling petals and an elegantly scrolled stem. Jerry looked at one design Constanza had just made on the paper. "We'll never be able to do that."

"Just stick to the crosses. They eat them either way."

"Hi, girls!" Sister Evangelina walked through

the door. "Sinta, Jerry." She nodded. "Oh, look! Thought I smelled something good."

"Oh yes, and you just happened along, Sister Evangelina. Don't try to be so innocent. I want you to bring some of these over to Padre when you take the host, all right? The rest are going to the country club."

"Are all those boxes you've got stacked over there going to the country club?"

"Yes. You got a problem with that?" Constanza asked.

"No problem, but those folks hardly ever show up in church."

"Eating hot-cross buns has absolutely nothing to do with going to church, Sister," Constanza said as she touched one of the buns to see if it was cool enough for the girls to start decorating.

"I know, I know . . . but it makes you wonder."

"Worried about them doing their Easter duty?"

Jerry looked apprehensively at her aunt, who seemed absorbed in her task of decorating the buns. She didn't like this talk of duty, going to church. She was pretty sure that her aunt didn't expect her to go. Still, all this talk made her nervous.

"I don't worry about them, but their children. I mean, all they think Easter is these days is Easter eggs and bunny rabbits."

"Easier than confession and Communion," Constanza offered. Jerry tried to concentrate on the buns. She couldn't exactly get up and leave. It would seem rude. And although she talked more now, she wasn't skillful enough to slide in and redirect the conversation, change the subject.

"Of course it's easier. Everything that's bad for you is easier."

"Chocolate rabbits aren't that bad for you."

"Constanza!" Sister Evangelina sighed. "I could use a little support here. I swear."

"Don't swear, Sister, it doesn't become a nun."

"I'll do anything I please." Sister Evangelina sniffed, and cast an eye toward the bowl of frosting.

Jerry shut her eyes, trying to block the talk. She was here, safe in her aunt's kitchen. There was the sweet smell of the hot-cross buns. There was this fat nun laughing at her aunt and her aunt teasing the nun. Jerry took up the pastry tube and focused on the newest batch of buns that had cooled and was now ready for decorating. She hardly heard what they were saying. Tomorrow was Good Friday.

She didn't know what she would do, if she would go to church or what. What had Zayana done? Prayed to all her gods—found room in her heart for the white lady, the Virgin; found room for the feathered serpent; found room for the eagle; found room for the words of the faith of her husband, León. But she, Jerry, was no Zayana. How could she ever be Zayana—Zayana, who had dragged that trunk from Quimpaco, to Tampico, to Mexico City—to Jerry! The thought was so startling. Could that be? Was this the meaning of it all? The trunk held mere things, but was she now the holder of Zayana's hopes?

Chapter 23

✦✦✦✦

We worship you, Lord,
we venerate your cross,
we praise your resurrection.
Through the cross you brought joy to the world.

May God be gracious and bless us;
And let his face shed its light upon us.
                                                (*Psalm 67:2*)

I T WAS LATE AFTERNOON on Good Friday, and Jerry stood next to Constanza outside, by the last cross in the churchyard. They had just completed the journey of the Stations of the Cross and were standing by the last station, the fourteenth, representing where Christ was laid in the tomb. Jerry liked the fact that they had done this outside. Sister Lucia, a nun from the same order as Sister Evangelina, had piped a soft melody on a wooden flute as the small congregation walked the stations. Padre Hernandez spoke the concluding words of the Veneration of the Cross. Jerry looked down and dug the toe of her shoe into the dirt and thin grass. A little piece of the earth seemed to move on its own to the left of her shoe. It was the silk-and-mud door of a trapdoor spider. The twilight hunters. She had never seen one or really looked for one since that first week. She remembered that it was the trapdoor spider that helped her speak aloud for the first time. *I hope they never get into your bread*. The words came back to her now. She could hear them so clearly in her head.

It was time now to go into the church again. Inside, the church was dark. There was not a flower decorating the altar, not a candle lit. The colorful altar cloths had been replaced with black draperies. Padre Hernandez genuflected and, raising the ciborium, spoke to the people: "This is the lamb of God who takes away the sins of the world. . . ."

It was getting dark when Jerry and Constanza were driving home from church. A purple light had settled over the land, and they had turned off down a dirt road to take a shortcut back to their house. The road was rough, for it had been badly cut up by arroyos. But the land was so beautiful that Jerry was happy because they had to go slow and happy that Constanza was driving and she could look out the window. The *chamisa* seemed to hover like mist rather than grow from the earth, and the spiky cacti stood like sentries against the mournful deep lavender sky. The road climbed up and Constanza pulled to the side where it widened. There was a broad gravel shoulder. She stopped the truck. The evening seemed steeped in the deep dusky purples that sometimes bled into the sky between twilight and night.

"First star!" Constanza said. And to Jerry the two words seemed like a prayer.

They opened the truck doors and stepped out.

Stars! Older than the stars. She remembered when she had tried to not think of stars. She had refused to write about that lovely passage from *Romeo and Juliet* just so she would not think about the stars—and Miriam who was older than the stars. This was in a sense the story of Jerry's life—trying not to think—and with it came silence, the immutable silence. And she had become so good at it. Why, yes, the first time she had ever seen

Constanza, when Constanza had unfolded those long legs from her truck and that dress swirled around her ankles in little gusts, Jerry hadn't even thought of her mother's skirt back then swirling around her ankles. She hadn't thought about her mom waving good-bye and the doll . . . the damn doll. It had all been perfect, a world of perfect silence. No sounds, no images got past her rating system. No sirree. The flawlessly mute world and she controlled it all. But now there were stars up there. Stars like little flames of candlelight. And Jerry pictured herself the obedient, silent small child standing by the window holding the candle. She pictured the sill, the one her mother was supposed to hoist herself over and come back through. She pictured herself waiting . . . waiting waiting. And then she tipped back her head and knew that she was no longer waiting. And she knew that she only wanted to see the stars and love them for what they were. The waiting was over. And the face of heaven was so fine that she loved the night with all its stars that now rose and shimmered over the mountains.

There was a doll. She had seen it from the first time she ever opened the trunk, but she hadn't ignored it, exactly. She had just decided not to think about it. She knew where the doll was. It was near where she had left the scrap of the map and the mezuzah. It hardly looked like a doll anymore. It had been gnawed on by rodents. The red dress had faded, and the little carved head that once probably had a painted face seemed worn smooth. Jerry lifted the lid of the trunk. The doll was there, faceless but waiting. Jerry thought of that girl on that far border of time with her veil of butterflies, and then numbly holding this very doll in her hands, not even knowing that she had a real live flesh-and-blood baby of her own. And she remembered her own mother now with her own dolls, the ones Jerry had tried not to think about. She picked up the doll and then replaced it very carefully. The doll was a doll, nothing more. Jerry felt something still in her. It was as if something had released deep within. She knew that she was not the first child to have a childish mother who confused her dolls with life. There was a medal, too, that she had seen. The medal had a flag on it and a date: January 6, 1912.

Time took a slow twist. She smelled sagebrush in the air. It smelled almost like home, but it wasn't home. There was a girl, maybe just a few years younger than herself, standing in a dress with a dropped waist and a flounced skirt and high-button shoes. . . .

In the House of the Schoolteacher
Via Roja
Vega del Monte
New Mexico
January 6, 1912

❖❖❖

Jeraldine

Because Papa is the schoolteacher, I must be perfect at the ceremonies. I have to recite the poem written by Papa's best friend, Señor Seña, also a schoolteacher. He wrote a poem to celebrate our becoming a state. Today is the day! Everyone is so excited. My brother, I think, is the most excited of all. Fernando is studying for the priesthood, and he says that this is the best thing that has happened in all of our lives. He says Señor Seña's poem captures the true meaning of statehood. I must confess I do not understand the poem at all. He keeps talking about now we have this new flag and it is unstained. So I ask unstained by what, and he says "blood"— the blood that came from the Spanish Inquisition.

But I still don't understand. I have lived here in Vega del Monte all twelve years of my life. I have seen no blood. I don't know what my brother is talking about, especially when he says *nuestra gente*, our people. . . . Which people is he speaking of ?

"Mama, Papa!" Fernando Morillo stood up at the table and began to lift a glass. "I know it has been a long day, a most wonderful day."

"Oh my goodness," Miguel Morillo smiled and reached for a cigar. "Already he speaks like a priest at a church fund-raiser. You see, my dear," he said, turning to his wife, "they get them started even before they are ordained."

A shadow of a grimace passed over Fernando's face. "No, Papa . . . this . . . this is . . ."

"Hush, Miguel," Mildred Morillo said. "Let our son go on."

"If I may," Fernando continued. "What I have to say may come as a shock, but . . ." He swallowed. Jeraldine was suddenly not sleepy. Something terrible, a sense of dread, seemed to have stolen into the room.

"Yes, go on," said his father somewhat sternly.

"Well, with the statehood of New Mexico, a time of new beginnings is at hand."

"Yes," said his mother warily.

Jeraldine had no idea what they were talking about, but her attention was riveted. "Mama, Papa"—he paused and looked over at his much-younger sister—"Jeraldine." Jeraldine glowed. She loved her big brother, and he included her the way adults never did. "Well, I have decided not to continue studying for the priesthood."

"You mean you have finished?" This time it was his grandmother Milagros who spoke.

"No, no, Abuela. I have not finished. I have stopped because I don't want to be a priest."

"What do you mean, Fernando?" Jeraldine asked. "How can I tell my friends at school this?"

"Your friends, Jeraldine? It is my life." The words were harsh but spoken gently. Jeraldine felt her eyes fill.

"We were all so proud, Fernando." It was as if his mother had sighed rather than actually spoken.

"There has always been a priest in this family, for generations." His Uncle Fernando spoke, his eyes cast down into the plate.

"That is just the problem." A tremor had crept into Fernando's voice.

"What are you talking about?" his mother asked.

"Mama, Papa, Uncle Nando, we have always had

priests in our family because we were scared. It was a cover, not a commitment. Faith by fear."

Uncle Fernando jumped up from the table and threw down his napkin. "I don't know what you're talking about. We have always been good Catholics."

Mildred Morillo's face turned pale, her eyes lifeless. She stared ahead into some lost space. "I know what he is saying and he better stop right now. It might be nineteen twelve, but it can happen again. It is safer to be Catholic."

Jeraldine suddenly exploded. "I don't understand what's going on here. I'm sick of being left out! What can happen again? Why is it safer to be Catholic? Isn't it the only way to be?"

Fernando turned slowly toward his young sister. "Not if you were not born that way."

"But you were, Fernando." His mother seemed to recover herself. "You were baptized." And she patted her head lightly. Fernando turned and walked out of the house. Jeraldine was frightened. She loved her big brother more than anything.

Fernando had not gone away for good. But he had moved out of the Casa de Hermanos, where the seminary students lived. He was living on the other side of the town, and Jeraldine had followed him one day to the house of a man.

"Fernando!" she called out.

"Jeraldine. What are you doing here?"

"I followed you. I had to tell you I don't care if you are a priest or not, as long as you are my brother. That is all that counts. But don't leave us." She gulped. She had sworn she would not cry. "Don't leave me."

"Jeraldine. I shall always be your brother. Nothing can change that and I am not leaving you. I am simply going *to* something."

"I don't understand."

"You will."

"I won't if no one tells me. What is this house? Who lives here?"

"A rabbi."

"A rabbi? You mean like a Jewish priest."

Fernando hesitated. "Yes."

"So you are going to be a priest!" Jeraldine said hopefully.

"No, Jeraldine. I am a Jew. I have always been a Jew and so have you."

My brother could not get rid of me. I stuck to him like a fly to flypaper. So he had no choice but to take me with him to the rabbi's house. I am sitting in the corner of the rabbi's study. Quiet as a mouse. The rabbi wears a long beard. I have never seen such a long beard. Somewhere in the crinkly whiskers that tumble like a waterfall down his shirt-front there is a mouth. I do not like the words the mouth says to my brother.

"You are not what you think you are. You have no proof." The voice is thick and sweaty sounding.

"But I have always been a Jew. What do you mean, proof that my family has kept the tradition? We couldn't."

"But many did secretly," the rabbi replies.

"But that is just the point, Rabbi: They had to do it secretly. So how could there be proof?"

"You must go to the mikvah, the ritual bath, and wash yourself of the impurities."

"But that is insulting. Don't you see that?"

"But only in that way can you convert."

"But I am not converting from anything. I have always been a Jew, in my heart, in my soul."

And round and round the argument goes. I'm tired. I'm very confused. I want my brother back—Jew or not. I fall asleep in the chair in the corner of the rabbi's study.

❖ ❖ ❖

How many more times did I see my brother? I do not remember. I just remember the last time. It was at twilight, and I had been waiting for him near the house where he now rented a room. He came out with a suitcase and started down the road toward the place where the bus stopped, the bus that went to Albuquerque and then west. They said it went all the way to California. I felt this terrible coldness fill my chest as I saw him walk out with his suitcase. I knew he was leaving for good. But it became one of those moments, those horribly long moments. There was this frightening clarity. Every blade of grass stood out. I could see a trapdoor spider lift its perfect little piece of earth and walk down toward the road. I could almost hear its eight little feet tamping in the dust. This was awful. My brother was leaving me, leaving *me* for a faith that would not have him!

Chapter 24

❖❖❖

JERRY'S HAND SHOOK. She looked down at the doll. Her mind was still with Jeraldine. She stood beside that girl in the dusty road. She stood beside her and tried to help her remember all the good things that her brother had done—the arms that had lifted her up to reach the fruit on the branches of the peach tree that grew in their backyard, the voice that had woven itself like silk through the long nights when she had had pneumonia, reading to her endless stories, fairy tales and myths. This was a myth, wasn't it, that was happening right now? Fernando was disappearing and then he would magically reappear. Yes, the peach from the tree would split open and Fernando would step out. Jerry shook her head. It was now Saturday. Holy Saturday. In a few hours she and Constanza would go to church for the service of light, the Easter vigil.

❖ ❖ ❖

"Amigos," Padre Hernandez welcomed them outside the church where a large fire burned. "Welcome on this our most holy night, when our Lord Jesus passed from death to life. We come together now in vigil and prayer. We honor the memory of his death and celebrate the resurrection. . . . We celebrate this holiest of the mysteries, and rejoice in that which cannot be fully understood but indeed brings the power of our Lord closer to us . . . and let us now pray as this fire is blessed from which we shall light the paschal candle. . . . Father, we share in the light of your glory through the light of your Son Jesus Christ. May blessings descend on this lighted candle and may the light from this fire inflame us with hope and love and may Almighty God and his son look down upon us through this light and shine through our long night, dispel the darkness and illuminate our souls. . . ."

Jerry closed her eyes tight. The fires would not diminish; huge bonfires blazed in her mind's eye. Bodies became ashes. The ashes swirled up into the sky. When Jerry and her aunt stepped out of the church after the service of the vigil, it was dark. The few stars that had begun to appear at twilight were beginning to vanish, their frail light sucked into the blackness of the night. Constanza walked slowly. A heaviness seemed to have settled upon her. She seemed smaller. It was as if she had shrunk within her own body and now was exhausted from dragging around something that was simply too large. Had she been wrong in telling Constanza all that she had discovered in the cellar? Was it simply too much for the old woman? They drove silently home. Constanza went straight to bed, hardly muttering a good night. Jerry watched as the door to her aunt's bedroom closed. She must go to the cellar now.

She descended the stairs. She knew it would be the last time. She lifted the lid of the trunk and picked up the corncob doll worn from its years of strange, obsessive, misplaced love.

❧ Jerry

I am stepping through a window of memory, my own memory. . . . When I stopped speaking, the words dropped away one by one, dropped away against a great wall of meaninglessness. Yes, one by one they dropped away and then there was silence. I did not have to hear my mother, not only her words unspeakable, although she spoke them, but her footsteps as she walked away, cradling her favorite doll. She had left the others for me. But still she walked away. No hesitancy, although she appeared to amble. That was her way—ambling. It was noon when Mother left me, and time seemed to stop. The sun congealed in a colorless sky. It was like a big yellow squawk and then there was silence. "Bye" was the first word I swallowed into that long silence. It simply froze on my lips as I watched my mom walk down the path to the road. I watched her until she grew into a dot, but oddly enough I felt as if I was the one who was vanishing into nothingness. There was this vast emptiness and it simply swallowed me into its silence. And that was all. My mother was gone.

So now I've told you about my mother and how the skirt, the stupid long skirt swirled around her ankles as she stood in the path and waved good-bye. . . .

Jerry set the corncob doll down. She felt a wind on her shoulder. It startled her. How could there be a draft down here in the cellar? And then she heard the creak of the stairs.

"Aunt Constanza?"

"Yes, dear, I'm coming down. It's time . . . it's time . . . it's time I looked in the trunk."

She came over to where Jerry knelt and folded her long legs until her knees looked pointy through the thin fabric of her skirt. Her hand darted out to a piece of paper Jerry had never even noticed that had stuck to the inside wall of the trunk. "That must be a page from Jeraldine's diary there, you know, my sister, your great-grandmother." Carefully she peeled off the paper. It was unreadable except for a few words.

"Her handwriting is just like yours, Aunt Constanza."

"Yes, but it's hers. Not mine. She was crazy as a bedbug. I told you that already. But smart. Smart as a whip. She had a sweet husband, part Navajo, part Tewa, too; that's how we're related to Margaret Santangel. They ran a gift shop up by the Santuario at Las Trampas. Good business, especially during Holy Week. Lot of people make pilgrimages there. They believe that the earth is *tierita bendit*, as they say—sacred earth, you know. Lot of Indians, including Margaret Santangel, believe in its healing powers. She gets her nephew to go over and dig it up."

"What does it heal?" Jerry asked.

"Oh." A dark light did a jig in Constanza's eyes. "I think it's just an old superstition."

A smile played across Jerry's face. "You do?"

Constanza shrugged her shoulders and looked up. "Who knows. Let's go up now."

They stood outside in the cook yard. Lacy clouds raced overhead and puffs of tumbleweed chased across the dry scrubland until fetching up on the *chamisa*. The breeze carried the scent of sagebrush, and Jerry and Constanza felt the warmth of the early sun of the new day on their faces. They heard a car coming down the road and saw a cloud of red dust rising.

"Oh Lord. Here comes Sister Evangelina." Constanza sighed.

Two minutes later Sister Evangelina pulled into the drive. She leaned out the window. "You don't look ready for church."

"We're not," Constanza replied.

"Well, get ready, dear; we'll be late. Easter Sunday after all."

"So it is," Constanza replied.

Sister Evangelina leaned farther out the window and peered hard at Constanza. "Constanza, what's going on with you?"

"Not much."

"Well, come on then."

"We're not going, Sister Evangelina." Jerry looked at her aunt. Was she really saying this? "Jerusalem and I are staying here."

Sister Evangelina looked completely confused. She started up the car. Then there was the sound of grinding gears and the car stopped. She leaned out the window again. "What did you just call your niece?"

"Jerusalem. I called her Jerusalem."

Epilogue

❖❖❖

T HE NAVAJOS BELIEVE that when the world was created, the people traveled through four worlds before climbing a reed from the bottom of the lake known as Changing Waters to this present world. They say that First Man and First Woman came with their first two children, who were called Changing Twins, and that they, First Man and First Woman, fashioned a mountain with their own hands from the earth, and they filled it with plants and animals. On the peak they placed a black bowl with two blackbird eggs in it. They held down the peak with a rainbow. One twin took some clay from a riverbed and made it into a bowl. The other twin found reeds growing and shaped them into a water basket. They picked up stones from the ground, and with these they chiseled axes, knives, spear points, and hammers.

Sometimes I feel like those First People. I feel as if I have climbed up through worlds, through windows in time. I have traveled to the edges of vast distances where borders are blurry and voices are muted. Through some mystery, through my silence, perhaps, I blew life into these people. They became animate. Their blood coursed, and as it did it coursed through me and I learned our secret. And here is a truth: In our secret selves we can grow old while we are still young; we can cross borders that no one else can see. We can hear voices that have long been silent. And that is what, I think, I have done.

Do you know how some people can see shapes in the clouds? Well, I see them in the shadows. The shadows cast by the clouds on the mountains or on the desert. The shadows become different when they are cast this way. They tell different stories. A cloud like a flying rabbit becomes a hooded figure in a shadow story, or perhaps an angel with wings.

Our family has the blood of many different peoples in its veins—Hispanics, both Jews and Catholics, and Indians, Aztec and Navajo and those of the pueblos. However, because of our long blood secret, I do not think that we come from the earth like the First People of the Navajo, nor from Adam's rib as the Bible says. I think we come from the shadowlands.

Descendants of Grazia Ribeiro

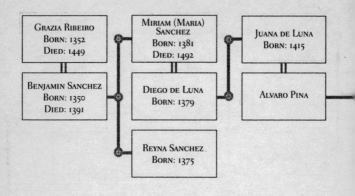

GRAZIA RIBEIRO
BORN: 1352
DIED: 1449

BENJAMIN SANCHEZ
BORN: 1350
DIED: 1391

MIRIAM (MARIA) SANCHEZ
BORN: 1381
DIED: 1492

DIEGO DE LUNA
BORN: 1379

REYNA SANCHEZ
BORN: 1375

JUANA DE LUNA
BORN: 1415

ALVARO PINA

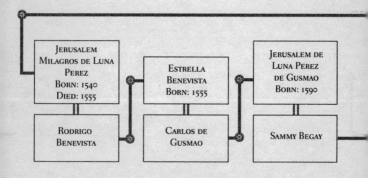

JERUSALEM MILAGROS DE LUNA PEREZ
BORN: 1540
DIED: 1555

RODRIGO BENEVISTA

ESTRELLA BENEVISTA
BORN: 1555

CARLOS DE GUSMAO

JERUSALEM DE LUNA PEREZ DE GUSMAO
BORN: 1590

SAMMY BEGAY

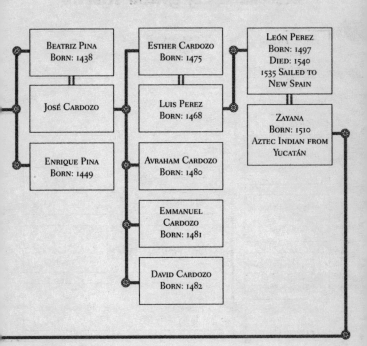

Descendants of Grazia Ribeiro

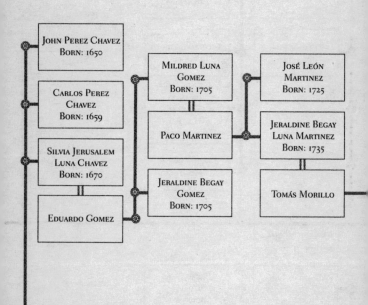

JOHN PEREZ CHAVEZ
BORN: 1650

CARLOS PEREZ
CHAVEZ
BORN: 1659

SILVIA JERUSALEM
LUNA CHAVEZ
BORN: 1670

EDUARDO GOMEZ

MILDRED LUNA
GOMEZ
BORN: 1705

PACO MARTINEZ

JERALDINE BEGAY
GOMEZ
BORN: 1705

JOSÉ LEÓN
MARTINEZ
BORN: 1725

JERALDINE BEGAY
LUNA MARTINEZ
BORN: 1735

TOMÁS MORILLO

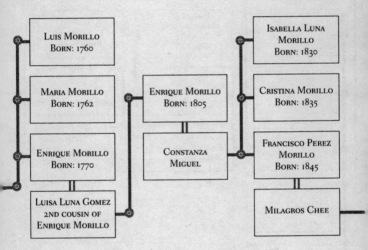

Descendants of Grazia Ribeiro

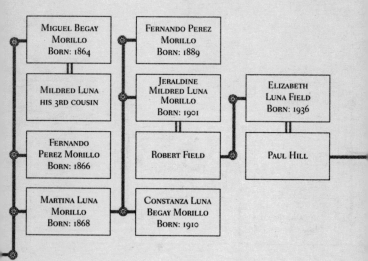

MIGUEL BEGAY
MORILLO
BORN: 1864

FERNANDO PEREZ
MORILLO
BORN: 1889

MILDRED LUNA
HIS 3RD COUSIN

JERALDINE
MILDRED LUNA
MORILLO
BORN: 1901

ELIZABETH
LUNA FIELD
BORN: 1936

FERNANDO
PEREZ MORILLO
BORN: 1866

ROBERT FIELD

PAUL HILL

MARTINA LUNA
MORILLO
BORN: 1868

CONSTANZA LUNA
BEGAY MORILLO
BORN: 1910

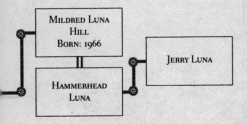

MILDRED LUNA
HILL
BORN: 1966

HAMMERHEAD
LUNA

JERRY LUNA

Author's Note

I FIRST BECAME INTERESTED in doing a novel about the Spanish Inquisition almost sixteen years ago when I read an article in the *New York Times* about the secret Jews of New Mexico and the Southwest. They were called crypto Jews. The ancestors of the secret Jews began coming to America as Conversos after they were expelled from Spain in 1492. It was not long before the Inquisition followed them to Mexico and they were forced to practice their religion covertly. After generations of spiritual subterfuge and repression, these Jews entirely forgot that they were Jews; indeed, they had become practicing Catholics, yet clung almost unwittingly to certain customs such as lighting candles on Friday night, not eating pork, and never mixing meat and dairy products.

In New Mexico these crypto Jews began to

intermarry over generations with other people of Spanish descent and the Indian populations as well. The story in the *New York Times* focused on a few of these people who were beginning to rediscover their heritage.

The Nazi holocaust took the lives of six million Jews within a period of a few years. In comparison, the number of lives, more than three hundred thousand, taken during the Spanish Inquisition was much smaller, but the most astonishing thing to me was the unimaginable stretch of time over which the Inquisition endured. The brutality that began with the burning of the Jewish quarter in Seville in 1391 persisted until 1826, when the last victim of the Inquisition died in Valencia, Spain. That an organized program for deadly persecution spanned nearly five hundred years is astounding. The madness that sustained such an endeavor is staggering to contemplate.

I knew that if I was to tell this story, I would have to tell the whole story—the centuries upon centuries saturated by blood. This story could not be told as a day in the life of the Inquisition, nor could it be the story of simply one family within one generation. The crushing weight of time would have to be as significant as any character. It took me ten years of thinking to figure out how I could try to encompass this dimension of time within a single book.

I do not think I would have ever attempted this book without the encouragement of my late editor, Meredith Charpentier. Patiently, quietly she waited and waited for me to begin the book. An editor cannot give a writer a voice, but a really great editor can quiet down a writer like myself and help her listen to the authentic voices in her own head. Meredith helped me listen for the voices that make up *Blood Secret*.

She died shortly after I completed the last draft of the book, and it is to her memory that I dedicate *Blood Secret*. She was my navigator through the shoals of this unbelievable history.

Cambridge, Massachusetts, March 2004

For Further Reading

Gerber, Jane S. *The Jews of Spain: A History of the Sephardic Experience*. New York: Free Press, 1992.

Marks, M. L. *Jews Among the Indians*. Chicago: Benison Books, 1992.

Netanyahu, Benzion. *The Origins of the Inquisition in Fifteenth-Century Spain*. New York: Random House, 1995.

Rochlin, Harriet and Fred. *Pioneer Jews: A New Life in the Far West*. Boston: Houghton Mifflin, 1984.

Roth, Cecil. *The Spanish Inquisition*. New York: W. W. Norton, 1937, 1964, 1996.

Sachar, Howard M. *Farewell España*. New York: Vintage, 1994.

Tobias, Henry J. *A History of the Jews in New Mexico*. Albuquerque: University of New Mexico Press, 1990, 1992.